NEVER STOP A GOOD FIGHT.

Suddenly Geraldine was there, pushing between them, her arms thrust out. "Stop this—do you hear me?" she pleaded.

"Go to hell, bitch," Orley snarled, and struck her.

Fargo caught her as she fell. She was doubled over in agony and didn't resist when he pushed her into a chair. Turning back, he felt hot fury course through his veins. He tore into Orley, a one-man hurricane, hammering him, beating down his guard, the thud of his blows like the beat of a drum.

"Help me!" Orley hollered.

Hector came to his friend's aid. He clipped Fargo on the ribs, caught him on the shoulder.

Furious, Fargo brought his right boot down on Hector's instep. Hector cursed and backpedaled, and Fargo went after him. Avoiding a left cross from Orley, he slammed two quick punches into Hector's belly. Hector bent over, putting his face in easy reach of Fargo's knee. Blood spurted, and Hector clutched at his nose. It was doubtful Hector saw the roundhouse right that brought him down.

Orley skipped back, less confident now that he was alone. "Hold on," he said as Fargo came toward him. "Let's call a truce."

"Let's not," Fargo said. He was in no mood to be merciful.

THE TRAILSMAN

#398

ARIZONA
AMBUSHERS

by

Jon Sharpe

A SIGNET BOOK

SIGNET
Published by the Penguin Group
Penguin Group (USA) LLC, 375 Hudson Street,
New York, New York 10014

USA | Canada | UK | Ireland | Australia | New Zealand | India | South Africa | China
penguin.com
A Penguin Random House Company

First published by Signet, an imprint of New American Library,
a division of Penguin Group (USA) LLC

First Printing, December 2014

The first chapter of this book previously appeared in *Riverboat Reckoning*, the three
hundred ninety-seventh volume in this series.

Copyright © Penguin Group (USA) LLC, 2014

REGISTERED TRADEMARK—MARCA REGISTRADA

ISBN 978-0-451-46906-9

Printed in the United States of America
10   9   8   7   6   5   4   3   2   1

The Trailsman

Beginnings . . . they bend the tree and they mark the man. Skye Fargo was born when he was eighteen. Terror was his midwife, vengeance his first cry. Killing spawned Skye Fargo, ruthless, cold-blooded murder. Out of the acrid smoke of gunpowder still hanging in the air, he rose, cried out a promise never forgotten.

The Trailsman they began to call him all across the West: searcher, scout, hunter, the man who could see where others only looked, his skills for hire but not his soul, the man who lived each day to the fullest, yet trailed each tomorrow. Skye Fargo, the Trailsman, the seeker who could take the wildness of a land and the wanting of a woman and make them his own.

1860, Arizona—where blood flows more freely than water, and death waits for the unwary.

1

Skye Fargo was a few miles out of Fort Bowie when he heard shots, a flurry of fifteen to twenty and then a few more, and then more.

Drawing rein, Fargo rose in the stirrups. A big man, broad of shoulder, he wore buckskins and a hat caked with the dust from the past week of long hours in the saddle. He placed his right hand on his Colt and cocked his head to listen.

A stillness gripped the arid Arizona countryside.

Fargo was passing through a range of low mountains. Boulders were more common than trees, and grass was sparse. The ground was parched for water as it always was in the summer. There wasn't a splash of green anywhere.

Fargo's lake blue eyes narrowed. A lot of gunshots nearly always meant trouble. A hunter seldom fired that many. That he was in the heart of Apache country—Chiricahua, to be exact—added to his unease.

With a tap of his spurs, Fargo rode on. The Ovaro pricked its ears, which told him the stallion heard something he didn't. Thanks to the twists and bends of the poor excuse for a road, he couldn't see more than a few hundred yards ahead.

Fargo held to a slow walk. He never took chances when Apaches might be involved. In his estimation they were about the deadliest warriors on the continent, and crafty as anything. He recollected hearing about the time some whites came on a horse picketed in the open and they rode up, thinking someone had left it there, only to have Apaches sprout out of the ground in ambush. The whites were lucky any of them survived.

Fargo rose in the stirrups again. He thought he'd heard a cry, of pain, maybe. It wasn't repeated, and he continued on with the hairs at the nape of his neck prickling.

It was a quarter of a mile before he rounded yet another bend and came on a straight stretch. At that point steep slopes pressed on the road from both sides. Anyone passing along the road would be a sitting duck for riflemen hidden above.

And that appeared to be exactly what had happened.

Fargo counted seven bodies. All wore uniforms. Three horses were down, as well. At first he thought it was a patrol out of the fort. But as he cautiously advanced, he spied a wagon on its side, in the brush at the side of the road. It had overturned when the driver tried to escape, was his guess.

The attack wasn't so much an ambush as a slaughter.

Drawing his Colt, Fargo scanned the slopes but saw no sign of the attackers. They were likely well away by now.

The first body he came on was a private. A boy, really, with a freckled face, and a bullet hole smack in the middle of his forehead.

Next were two soldiers sprawled close together.

Fargo noticed that one had a hole on the right side of his head. The other had been shot in the left temple.

The soldiers hadn't stood a prayer, not with enemies on both sides.

Close by, someone groaned.

Drawing rein, Fargo swung down. He moved toward where he believed the sound came from and saw a pair of boots and then legs sticking out of brown grass.

The man was on his back, his hat off, a hand pressed to a scarlet stain on his shirt, his face contorted in pain. Another groan escaped him.

Quickly, Fargo knelt. Only then did he notice the insignia on the uniform. "Major?" he said, touching the officer's shoulder. "Can you hear me?"

The officer's eyelids fluttered. He gazed blankly about, as if unsure of where he was, then focused on Fargo and seemed to come to his senses. "Who?" he gasped.

Fargo told him, adding, "I'm a scout. On my way to the fort."

"Massacred us," the major said with great effort. "Cut us down like dogs." He took a deep breath. "My men?"

"I haven't checked them all yet but you appear to be the only one still breathing." And it wouldn't be for long, Fargo reflected. "Who attacked you? How many were there?"

"Didn't see . . . anyone," the major got out, and quaked.

That sounded like Apaches to Fargo.

The major moved a finger, touching his chest. "I'm Major Waxler. Paymaster. This was my detail."

Fargo glanced at the overturned wagon. "Paymaster?" he repeated. "How much is in the wagon?"

Waxler had to try twice to answer. "Thirty thousand dollars. Most in silver and gold coins."

"I'll fetch you some water," Fargo said, and went to rise to get his canteen.

"No." The major grabbed Fargo's wrist. "Check on the others first. Please."

Fargo nodded. He quickly went from trooper to trooper, confirming each was dead, and came to the wagon. The driver hung from the seat, the lower half of his face a ruin. Gripping a wheel, Fargo clambered up. The door had been flung wide. He peered in, and grunted. The wagon was empty.

Jumping down, Fargo returned to Waxler. The major's eyes were closed. Hunkering, Fargo gripped his hand. "Major?"

Waxler looked at him. "My men?"

Fargo shook his head.

"The payroll?"

Fargo shook his head a second time. "Was it in a strongbox?"

"Bags," the major wheezed.

Fargo frowned. That would have made it easier for whoever took the money. "I'll get you that water now."

"No need," Major Waxler said. "I'm about done for."

Fargo didn't say anything. He refused to offer false hope.

The major gazed at the sky as if searching for something. "Will you do me a favor?"

"Anything."

"Ask the colonel at Fort Bowie to get word to my wife."

"He'll do that anyway," Fargo said.

"I've only been married a short while," Waxler said, and coughed. A drop of blood appeared at the corner of his mouth. "I love her dearly."

Fargo would rather hear about the attackers. "Isn't there anything you can tell me about who ambushed you?"

"Geraldine will be crushed," Waxler said as if he hadn't heard. "She's so taken by her new life. To have it nipped in the bud . . ." He coughed again and a second drop dribbled after the first.

"The men who ambushed you," Fargo prompted.

"I told you," Major Waxler said. "We never saw them. Except

3

Private Etherage." Waxler sucked in the deepest breath yet. "He was driving the wagon. Just before the shooting started, he looked up and cried a warning." Waxler's brow knit. "Now that I think about it, it was a strange."

"How so?"

"His exact words were"—Waxler paused—" 'Look up there. Is that who . . .' "

"That's all?" Fargo asked when the major didn't go on.

"All," Waxler said, barely above a whisper. His body seemed to fold in on itself. He looked at the sky once more, said softly, "Geraldine, I'm so sorry." And breathed his last.

"Damn," Fargo said. Rising, he debated. He hated to leave the bodies for the buzzards to get at but there weren't enough horses left to carry all of the dead troopers. The smart thing was to hurry to the fort and let the commander know so a detail could be sent right out.

Stepping to the Ovaro, Fargo hooked his boot in the stirrup and forked leather. He was about to flick the reins when he caught movement out of the corner of his eye, high up. Instantly, he palmed his Colt but saw no one. He waited, worried that the Apaches were still up there and had him in their sights. Yet if that was the case, they'd have shot him by now.

After a minute went by and nothing happened, Fargo brought the stallion to a fast walk. To go faster in that blistering heat would exhaust the Ovaro before they got there.

Fargo holstered his Colt and thought of the dead troopers. As bad as the slaughter had been, he'd seen a lot worse. At least the paymaster and his men hadn't been mutilated. Or been taken alive and carved on.

Fargo was one of the few who didn't entirely blame the Apaches for the state of grisly affairs. Decades ago, Mexico had placed a bounty on Apache scalps, and scalp hunters from both sides of the border had killed scores of Apache women and children for the few miserable coins on their hair. Sometimes the scalp hunters killed friendly Indians from other tribes and claimed the scalps were Apache.

Then there was that incident some years back where a trader had invited a peaceful band of Apaches to a feast. Once the Apaches were gathered around the food, the trader and his men opened up on them with rifles and a cannon.

Was it any wonder, Fargo reflected, that the Apaches killed every white and Mexican they came across?

The thud of the Ovaro's hooves was the only sound in all that vast emptiness.

By his reckoning Fargo had less than a mile to go when he crested a hill.

Someone was coming toward him.

Drawing rein, Fargo sat rooted in amazement.

It was a slim woman on a sorrel. She was dressed all in pink, including a pink hat, with a pink parasol held aloft to shield her from the worst of the sun.

The woman spotted him and straightened but kept on coming. As she neared, Fargo saw that the pink hat had a pink feather. Placing his hands on his saddle horn, he said in greeting, "Howdy, ma'am."

The woman didn't answer.

As she came up she regarded him coldly. Her eyes were the russet brown of acorns, the long hair that cascaded past her shoulders the same color. She had an oval face, wide across the brow and pointed at the chin, and nice lips.

"Hold on, there," Fargo said.

She did no such thing. It was apparent she intended to ride on by without speaking.

Fargo wheeled the Ovaro to block her way. "Didn't you hear me, lady?"

The woman in pink scowled and drew rein. She still didn't say a word.

"You don't want to go that way," Fargo said.

All she did was stare.

"There are Apaches yonder," Fargo said, pointing back the way he came. "I'm trying to save your hide." He figured she would finally say something, maybe thank him for stopping her.

Instead, she closed her parasol, raised her right arm, and pointed a derringer at his head.

2

Skye Fargo froze in his saddle. At that range the woman could hardly miss.

"Move your horse and let me pass," she demanded.

"Didn't you hear me about the Apaches?"

"I'm not afraid of them."

"You should be, lady," Fargo said. "They'll kill you as quick as they'll kill a man. Or maybe you'll get lucky and one of them will take you for his own." Although as Fargo well knew, Apache warriors generally held white women in low regard because they were too soft to adapt to the Apache way of life.

"I won't tell you again," the woman said. "If you think I won't shoot, you're mistaken. I've squeezed the trigger on stupid bastards before."

"I'm stupid for trying to help you?"

"So you claim," the woman said. "But if there's one thing I know about men, you're all a pack of liars." She paused, then added, "Almost all of you, anyhow."

Fargo felt his temper rise. "Lady, a few miles back a paymaster and his men were wiped out and—" He got no further.

The woman's eyes widened. She uttered a loud gasp, and before he could guess her intent, she reined sharply to the side of the road to get past him, slapped her legs against her sorrel, and broke into a gallop.

Fargo went after her. He had no idea why she was behaving so strangely. By rights, he should let her get herself killed since she wouldn't listen to reason. Instead, he swore and used his spurs.

Her tresses flying, the lovely figure in pink was riding like a madwoman. She still had the derringer in her hand; it gleamed now and then in the bright sun.

Fargo kept her in sight but didn't try to overtake her. For one thing, the Ovaro was tired, and for another, while the woman had lost her head, he hadn't lost his, and he'd like to keep it that way. One of them should keep their eyes peeled for Apaches.

After about a mile and a half the sorrel began to flag, as Fargo reckoned would happen. As hot as it was, about two miles was the limit for a horse at a gallop. The woman should stop and let hers rest a while but she showed no inclination to do so.

Fargo swore some more. Some people had only a thimbleful of brains, if that. He held to a trot, refusing to exhaust the Ovaro because of her stupidity.

Another half a mile and the sorrel was plainly winded. It had slowed, even though the woman was hitting it with her parasol and smacking its legs.

It wouldn't be long now, Fargo told himself.

It wasn't. The lathered sorrel came to a halt. Head down, nostrils flaring, it wheezed like a bellows.

The woman in pink was jerking on the reins and saying anxiously, "Get along, there! Get along!" when Fargo came up. Shifting in her saddle, she pointed the derringer. "You again."

"I have a soft spot for idiots."

"I told you to stay away. I don't need your help."

"It's not you I'm thinking of," Fargo said, and nodded at the sorrel. "It's your animal. You pushed too hard. It's about wore out."

The woman glanced at the Ovaro. "Yours isn't, I see."

"I'm not as dumb as you."

Her features hardened and she wagged the derringer. "Get down."

"What?" Fargo said in surprise.

"You heard me. I'm taking your horse and going on."

"They call that horse stealing," Fargo said. "In these parts men get hung for it."

"I'm not a man, and under the circumstances anyone would understand." She wagged the derringer more forcibly. "Get down, I say. Don't make me shoot you."

"You're making a mistake, lady," Fargo said. "The last person who stole my horse, I shot to pieces."

"If you're trying to scare me, it won't work. Now dismount, damn you."

Fargo felt his jaw muscles twitch. There was a limit to how much he would abide. Wrapping his reins around his saddle horn, he began to swing his leg up and over.

7

The woman, taking it for granted he was going to do as she wanted, looked off down the road.

Fargo exploded into motion. Pushing off the saddle, he slammed into her, his arm going around her waist even as he grabbed her wrist to prevent her from shooting him. The impact knocked her from her saddle, and they tumbled to the ground. She managed to twist as they fell, and they both came down hard on their sides. Where most women might have screamed or clawed at him, she grunted, then tried to ram her knee between her legs.

Fargo took the blow on his thigh. Rolling, he straddled her, or tried to. She struggled fiercely, bucking like a mustang. Her free arm flashed, and she punched him on the chin. Grabbing her wrist, he pressed both her arms to the ground. "Calm down, damn you."

She did no such thing. Hissing in fury, she slammed a knee into his back close enough to his spine to send pain clear up to his neck.

Fargo tried one last time. "I won't tell you again."

She didn't listen. Arching her body, she sought to throw him off, and when she couldn't, she tried to sink her teeth into his wrist to free her gun hand.

Fargo had taken all he was going to. Balling his fist, he slugged her, almost as hard as he'd hit a man. Her head snapped back and her eyelids fluttered but she didn't pass out. Quickly, he wrested the derringer from her grasp, and stood. "It's over, lady. Now behave yourself."

The woman rose onto her elbows and glared. "Give me that."

"Not a chance in hell," Fargo said. "I'm taking you to Fort Bowie whether you want to go or not."

"Not a chance in hell," she mimicked him, and kicked at his knee.

Fargo barely dodged. He was strongly temped to slug her again but settled for pointing her derringer at her. "That's enough out of you."

"You won't shoot me," she brazenly declared, sitting up. "Kill a woman and you'll be hung."

"Not when the woman is as loco as you."

Ignoring him, she rose and swiped at dirt on her dress. "I'm going on with or without my derringer and there's nothing you can do to stop me."

"I can tie you over your saddle."

She looked at him, and somehow Fargo had the sense that she was seeing him for the first time. Until now, she had been concerned only about whatever it was that had driven her to nearly ride her horse into the ground. "Look," she said, "I realize you're trying to help. I appreciate that. I truly do."

"You have a hell of a way of showing it."

To his surprise, she blushed. "It's just that . . ." She didn't finish.

"What?"

"I have to go on."

"Damn, you're stubborn."

"Please," she said, and there was no denying her plea was genuine. "Take me to where the paymaster and his men were attacked. Do that, and afterward I'll gladly go with you to the fort."

"Wait a minute." Fargo glanced in the direction of the slaughter and then at the woman and then off toward Fort Bowie. "You were coming from the fort when I met you."

"I was," she said.

"You were riding to meet the detail?"

"I was," she said again, and her voice broke slightly.

Insight dawned, and Fargo wanted to kick himself. "You're married to one of the men."

"I'm Major Waxler's wife."

"Then you must be Geraldine."

She stiffened and suddenly stepped up and placed her hands on his chest, her eyes filling with tears. "You talked to him? He was alive when you found him?"

"For a little bit," Fargo said, and felt a pang of regret at hitting her. "You were all he thought of at the end."

Geraldine Waxler bowed her head and uttered a soft sob.

"I'm sorry," Fargo said. He started to raise an arm to put it around her shoulders to comfort her, but she turned her back to him and went on sobbing. He moved off a short way to let her weep in peace.

In the distance a hawk soared high in the sky.

Fargo should have suspected the truth sooner. No one did what she'd done without good cause. He stared into the heat haze until he heard the rustle of her dress.

"I'm sorry." Geraldine had wiped her face with a handkerchief and reclaimed her parasol.

"You have nothing to apologize for."

"I'd still like to go see."

"It's not a pretty sight."

"I wouldn't expect it to be," Geraldine said.

Fargo tried one last time. "They'll bring the bodies back to the fort. You can see him then."

"Please."

Fargo looked into those wonderful eyes of hers, now twin pools of sorrow, and swore.

"Thank you," Geraldine said.

"I didn't say I would," Fargo said, although he knew as well as she did that he'd given in.

"I'll be quick about it. I promise." Geraldine's throat bobbed. "I just have to see him."

"We're talking *Apaches*," Fargo reminded her.

"I'm well aware of the risk. And that it's unfair of me to ask you to put your life in danger. Head for Fort Bowie and I'll go on alone."

"You want me to just ride off? What do you take me for?"

"A decent man."

"Hell." Fargo stepped to the sorrel and held out his hand to her. "Come on. I'll give you a boost up. Let's get this over with."

"You're coming with me?"

"Did you really think I wouldn't?"

Geraldine smiled in gratitude. "I just hope I don't get you killed."

"Makes two of us," Fargo said.

3

Given their uncanny knack for finding anything dead to feed on, human or otherwise, Fargo wasn't surprised to see over a dozen buzzards circling above the ambush site.

"Oh, Lord," Geraldine Waxler exclaimed in horror. "Those are vultures."

"Yes, ma'am." Fargo had his hand on his Colt. For all he knew, the attackers might be somewhere near.

"It will be ghastly, won't it?"

"It won't be pretty. Are you sure you want to go through with this?"

Geraldine grimly nodded. "I owe it to Hank."

"He told me you were only married a short while."

"Six months," Geraldine said.

"That's all?"

"Why do you sound surprised? Because I insist on seeing his body?" Geraldine didn't wait for him to answer. "It's not how long someone is married that counts. It's how deeply they love each other."

Fargo didn't have much experience in that regard. His dealings with women usually consisted of a tumble under the sheets, and off he went.

"I loved Hank with all my heart," Geraldine went on. She let a few moments go by and said, "But listen to me. He's not even buried and I talk about him as if he's a thing of the past."

"You're young," Fargo said to console her. "You'll find someone else someday."

"I don't want anyone else." Geraldine frowned. "And I might not look it but I'm pushing thirty. If you think that's young, you're sadly mistaken."

"It's not old," Fargo said.

"In my profession it was."

"What did you do?" Fargo asked, more to hold up his end of the conversation than anything.

"None of your damn business."

Puzzled by the venom in her tone, Fargo glanced over and saw her stiffen. She was staring up ahead. He looked, thinking she had seen more buzzards feeding on the dead.

Three Apaches were standing near the overturned wagon, watching them approach. All wore headbands and moccasins, and cradled rifles.

Fargo drew rein. Geraldine, thankfully, did the same. He was about to unlimber his Colt when he realized the Apaches weren't resorting to their rifles. The warriors just stood there, staring.

"It's them!" Geraldine exclaimed. "The savages who killed my Hank. Do something."

"Hold on," Fargo said.

The Apaches showed no concern whatsoever. As casually as

11

if they were on a Sunday stroll, they turned and went around the wagon.

Fargo waited for them to reappear at the other end or to see them climb the slope. But they did neither.

"What are you waiting for?" Geraldine demanded. "Go after them."

"There are three of them and one of me." Fargo wasn't about to rush into their gun muzzles.

"We can't let them get away."

"We?" Fargo was looking for sign of more warriors.

"Damn you," Geraldine spat, and the next moment her derringer was in her hand, and she jabbed her heels.

"Hell." Fargo took off after her. He caught up just as she reached the wagon. Lunging, he grabbed her bridle but she was out the saddle before he could stop her, and darted around the wagon. "Don't!" he cried, afraid he would hear the blast of gunfire and see her crumple to earth. But no shots rang out.

Vaulting down, Fargo ran after her.

Geraldine had stopped and was looking around in confusion. "There's no one here. Where did they get to?"

Fargo was as amazed as she was, and shouldn't be. He'd dealt with Apaches before. They were will-o'-the-wisps, masters at melting away as if they were never there.

"Where *are* they?" Geraldine said again. "I saw them as plain as anything."

"We have to light a shuck," Fargo urged. At any moment, those warriors might jump them.

"I'm not leaving until I've seen my husband."

"If you're trying to get us killed," Fargo said, "you're going about it the right way."

"I told you not to come with me," Geraldine said, wheeling and striding past him. "I could have done this myself."

To get it over with, Fargo said, "Let me show you where he is."

Apaches were notorious for their horse stealing so Fargo took the Ovaro and the sorrel along.

Geraldine appeared to be disappointed that she had no one to shoot. "All they did was stare at us."

"You don't know when you're well off." Fargo was growing annoyed by her thickheadedness.

"I just don't understand. Apaches are bloodthirsty monsters. Everybody knows that. Yet they haven't tried to kill us."

"We stick around long enough, they might change their minds."

"You're not the least bit funny."

"Who's trying to be?" Fargo came to a halt.

"Why did you stop?"

Fargo pointed at the mortal remains of the late Major Henry Waxler. "Isn't he why we're here?"

Geraldine gasped and put a hand to her throat. Rushing over, she dropped to her knees. "Hank! Oh, Hank," she cried, and buried her face in his shoulder.

One thing Fargo could say, the woman wasn't squeamish. She didn't seem to mind that the vultures had been at her beloved. One eye had been plucked out, and the major's nose and a cheek were in strips and pieces.

Geraldine commenced to sob, deeply and bitterly.

All Fargo could do was wait her grief out. He stood guard, acutely aware that any moment might bring the crash of guns and the yip of war whoops. He was as mystified as Geraldine as to why the Apaches lit out like they did. It was out of character for them to slaughter the detail, then let a lone man and woman live.

Eventually, Geraldine's sobs dwindled to groans and sniffles. Raising her head, she dabbed at her eyes with her handkerchief. "I am about cried out."

"Then let's fan the breeze."

"I want to take Hank with us."

"The soldiers at the fort will bring all the bodies back." Fargo hankered to get out of there while they still could. He was sure unseen eyes were on them.

"When? Tomorrow? The day after?" Geraldine shook her head. "By then there won't be much left. We take him with us or I don't go."

Once again Fargo's temper flared. "It will slow us down."

"Not if you put Hank over my horse and let me ride double with you."

Fargo would just as soon throw *her* over her horse, but he gave in. The sooner they were under way, the better. In swift order he hoisted the major onto the sorrel, belly down, and ran rope under the sorrel, from Waxler's wrists to his ankles, to keep the body from sliding off.

Swinging onto the Ovaro, Fargo held out his hand to Geraldine. She clambered on without a word and looped an arm around his waist.

"Thank you," she said in his ear.

Fargo didn't breathe easy until they'd gone a half mile, and even then, he checked behind them, often.

13

Geraldine was unusually quiet. He'd given her the lead rope to hold, and she must have put a crick in her neck staring sorrowfully at her husband's body.

"He was lucky to have a woman like you," Fargo remarked at one point.

"What makes you say that?" she asked without taking her gaze from the major.

"I've met women who didn't give a good damn if their husbands lived or died," Fargo said. "You cared for yours."

"I'll never forget what he did for me."

"A lot of officers get hitched."

"Not to me they wouldn't."

Fargo wondered what she meant by that. "It's not as if you're hard on the eyes."

"I thank you for the compliment but that's not what I meant. We all have secrets, and mine are darker than most."

Fargo snorted. "How bad can they be?"

Geraldine started to say something, and gazed back down the road. "Say, is that dust yonder?"

Damned if it wasn't, Fargo saw with a start. A cloud of it, raised by riders. Since it hadn't been there the last time he looked, whoever was raising the dust must have come out of the wild country beyond.

"Are those Apaches after us?"

Fargo brought the Ovaro to a trot. It was a long way to the fort and he wanted to stay ahead of whoever was back there.

"I never expected any of this when I decided to surprise Hank," Geraldine remarked.

"When was he due at Fort Bowie?"

"By this evening sometime at the latest," Geraldine answered. "Why?"

Fargo had hoped that if the pay wagon was late, the fort's commander might already have sent out a patrol to find out why.

"We'll make it, won't we? Or is there something you're not telling me?"

"We'll make it," Fargo said, trying to sound convincing.

The dust cloud had swelled in size.

"I've lost my husband, and now this," Geraldine said. She faced front, stiffened, and pointed again. "Say, is that what I think it is?"

Fargo swore, and drew rein.

More dust was coming their way.

4

"Apaches behind us and now Apaches in front of us?" Geraldine Waxler said in alarm. "What do we do?"

"We sit tight." Fargo had caught glimpses of the riders up ahead. They were wearing uniforms. As they approached he counted ten soldiers. Not nearly enough when dealing with Apaches but ten were better than none.

"Are those hats?" Geraldine said. The obvious occurred to her, and she exclaimed, "Oh! They're troopers. They must be on their way to meet my husband's detail."

That's what Fargo, thought, too.

The soldiers clattered to a stop at the command of the officer leading them.

Lieutenant William Bremmer smiled in greeting. "Skye Fargo, as I live and breathe. How long has it been? A year or more?"

"At least," Fargo said.

"No one told me that you've been assigned to Fort Bowie." Bremmer was a couple of years out of West Point, a career man whose abiding passion was the army. On the stocky side, he had curly hair and freckles that he hated.

"I'm bringing a dispatch," Fargo said. The army had needed a seasoned rider to make it through, and scouts were the most seasoned of all.

"Ah." Lieutenant Bremmer turned to Geraldine and his smile disappeared. "Mrs. Waxler," he said coldly. "You're the reason we're out in this god-awful heat. You left the fort without permission. Colonel Chivington is most perturbed. He . . ." Bremmer stopped. He'd noticed the sorrel behind the Ovaro. "Dear God. Is that a body?"

"My husband," Geraldine said.

"The paymaster and his men were wiped out," Fargo informed him.

Bremmer didn't hide his shock. He recovered quickly, though, and sent a soldier back to the fort to have them send more men. He also assigned a pair of troopers to escort Geraldine and her dead husband back. "As for you, Skye, I'd like you to take us to where the attack took place."

Fargo sighed.

Geraldine held out her hand to him. "This is where we part company, then. I want to thank you for all you've done."

Fargo grinned as he shook. "Someone didn't give me much choice." He watched her ride off with both relief and mild regret.

"Are you ready?" Lieutenant Bremmer said.

Fargo was tired and hungry and by rights should get the dispatch through, but a short delay wouldn't matter much. He wheeled the Ovaro and saw that the dust cloud behind them was fading. "There are Apaches about," he warned. "We saw three."

"Those damnable fiends," Lieutenant Bremmer said. "They were to blame, then?"

"Who else, sir?" a sergeant piped up. "They're the scourge of the territory."

Once again, Fargo made for the ambush site. The blistering sun and the dust added to his thirst; he dearly craved a whiskey or three.

Lieutenant Bremmer cleared his throat. "So tell me. How did you become entangled in Mrs. Waxler's web?"

"Her what?" Fargo said.

"An apt description, I should think," Bremmer said, "for a former hussy."

"Hussy?"

"You don't know, then, about her past?"

"I only just met the lady."

"*Lady* is a stretch. You see, not all that long ago, Mrs. Waxler made her living by spreading her legs for any man with a few coins in his pocket."

"How's that?" Fargo said in surprise.

"Need I spell it out? Especially for a man like you?" The lieutenant chuckled. "Your fondness for females is as well-known as your fondness for liquor."

"Well, hell," Fargo said. "But what's this about Geraldine?"

"Her maiden name is Broganbush. To be blunt, she was a notorious Tucson prostitute. They say her charms are considerable. They must be, given how easily she snared that poor fool Hank Waxler."

16

"Why a fool?" Fargo asked.

"Aren't you paying attention? He married a whore. What man in his right mind does such a thing?"

"You think she tricked him into it?"

"To be honest, I doubt much deception was involved. From what I hear, Waxler was smitten at the sight of her. He actually got down on his knees next to the bed she'd slept in with a hundred men and proposed. Or so the story goes."

"He must have been in love," Fargo said.

"I call it rank stupidity," Lieutenant Bremmer said. "But don't get me wrong. He was a fine officer. A bit staid and humorless, as I recall. But to marry a woman like her. I never knew he had a romantic bone in his body."

Fargo shrugged. "Waxler was a grown man. He could do as he pleased."

"Within certain limits, yes. But he was an officer. He should have shown better judgment. As it was, for a while he became the talk of the mess hall. The men were laughing at him behind his back. He knew they were, yet strangely, he didn't seem to care."

Fargo rose in the stirrups. If the Apaches had been after them, they were gone now. Maybe the warriors had spied the soldiers and made themselves scarce.

"I wanted to ask him about it, but it was hardly my place," Bremmer related. "And now I'll never find out why he was willing to marry someone with so unsavory a reputation."

Fargo wished that the lieutenant would stop yammering. It was none of his damn business what the major did or why the major did it.

"How do you feel about it?"

"I don't."

"You must have an opinion one way or the other."

"I don't judge folks," Fargo set Bremmer straight. "Not when it comes to things like that."

"When do you judge, then?" Bremmer wanted to know.

"When a hard case or a hostile is out to put windows in my skull or buck someone out in gore."

"That's not the kind of judging I'm talking about," Bremmer said. "You're deliberately avoiding the question."

"Like hell."

They were crossing a flat stretch, with yucca and a few cactus on either side. Typical Arizona countryside, yet for some reason Fargo felt a tingle of apprehension, as if something were amiss.

"No need to be so prickly," Lieutenant Bremmer said. "I was only speaking my mind. You'll find that a lot of the officers agree with me. Hank Waxler made a mistake marrying that Jezebel. Now that he's gone, she'll most likely return to her old profession."

Fargo was on the verge of telling Bremmer that he'd listened to all he was going to about the paymaster and his new wife, when the bare earth near a yucca seemed to move. He blinked, not sure he had seen what he thought he had, and his moment of indecision proved costly.

Like the dead rising from cemetery graves, swarthy figures heaved up out of the earth. Only these were alive, and pressed rifles to their shoulders even as several let out with wolfish war whoops.

"Apaches!" an enlisted man screamed.

Fargo already had his Colt out and up. He fired at a warrior taking aim at Bremmer, swiveled, and shot another rushing toward them.

Rifles blasted to the right and the left.

A glance showed Fargo that several troopers had been shot from their saddles. "Ride!" he bawled. If they didn't, they'd suffer the same fate as the paymaster's detail.

Bending low, Fargo resorted to his spurs.

"Listen to Fargo!" Lieutenant Bremmer bawled. "As you value your lives men, ride!"

The survivors were quick to follow suit.

Fargo was surprised the Apaches didn't give chase. Another glance revealed that Bremmer and five others were hard on his heels, one of the latter reeling.

A few slugs were sent after them but most of the Apaches were converging on the soldiers they'd shot.

Lieutenant Bremmer quickly caught up. "We can't leave those men back there. We have to turn back."

"I counted eleven Apaches," Fargo shouted, in order to be heard above the drum of hooves.

"I don't care." The young officer raised an arm and began to slow and his men did likewise.

Reluctantly, Fargo did the same. He very much doubted any of the fallen soldiers were still alive.

"Men!" Bremmer yelled. "We must save who we can. Private Jackson, you stay here. You're wounded. The rest of us will charge the hostiles and drive them off."

"Just the few of us?" a trooper said skeptically.

"Plus the scout," Bremmer said.

"It's not enough," another soldier said, and pointed to the west. "Look!"

Riders were sweeping toward them. This time they didn't wear hats. They wore headbands.

"More Apaches!" a trooper exclaimed.

Fargo couldn't tell how many there were. It didn't matter. They were greatly outnumbered. "You want my advice?" he said to Bremmer. "We ride like hell."

"But the farther we go, the harder it will be to circle back to the fort," Bremmer objected.

"We can stay here and be wiped out, if that's what you want."

Bremmer scowled. "It's just not in my nature to tuck tail, is all."

"Is it in your nature to die?"

The men were anxiously awaiting their officer's decision. One, more nervous than the rest, muttered, "Come on, come on, will you? Make up your mind."

"We ride," Lieutenant Bremmer ordered, "and hope to God there aren't more Apaches up ahead."

Fargo didn't say anything, but there might well be.

5

The overturned wagon, the bodies, everything was as it had been.

Fargo was out of the saddle before the troopers. Shucking his Henry from its scabbard, he levered a cartridge into the chamber and faced back the way they had come.

The only dust in the air was their own.

"Where are the Apaches?" Lieutenant Bremmer wondered, joining him. "This is a good spot to make a stand."

"Is it?" Fargo said, gesturing.

Bremmer studied the flanking slopes and nodded. "I see what you mean."

The other troopers were helping Private Jackson off his mount. Pale as a sheet and dripping sweat, Jackson gritted his teeth as they carefully laid him down.

"Where's Sergeant Tilman?" Lieutenant Bremmer asked. "I didn't see what happened to him."

"He took a slug in the head, sir," a trooper replied. "He was one of the first those devils shot."

"Damn the luck," Bremmer said. "Very well. Let's see what we can do for Jackson."

Fargo was left on his own. Going to the overturned wagon, he climbed on top for a better view. There was no sign of the Apaches. Either they had decided the soldiers weren't worth the bother or they had something else in mind. That "something else" bothered him.

Private Jackson bleated in pain; Bremmer was probing the wound, trying to find the lead.

Fargo tried to imagine himself in the Apaches' moccasins. There were two things Apache warriors prided themselves on. One was to steal without being caught, the other to kill without being killed. Those were the closest Apaches came to having a commandment to live by.

With that in mind, Fargo reckoned there was only one thing the Apaches would do. And why not, when the whites had fallen for it once? Jumping down, he returned to the others.

"Lordy, it hurts," Private Jackson was saying. He was a young one, another green-behind-the-ears boy expected to hold his own against formidable killers like the Chiricahuas.

"Quit your squirming," Lieutenant Bremmer said. "I can't feel it if you keep moving around." His finger was in the bullet hole.

"I feel sick," Jackson said.

"Don't you dare," Bremmer replied. "I'll make you wash and clean my uniform."

"I've been shot!"

"That's no excuse."

Fargo supposed the lieutenant was trying to be funny, but no one laughed. "We don't have all day," he warned. "We need to light a shuck."

"First things first." Lieutenant Bremmer wore a look of intense concentration. He moved his hand and everyone heard the squish of his finger. "What's this? I think I've found it."

Bending, Fargo hiked his pant leg, revealing a sheath strapped to his ankle, and an Arkansas toothpick. He offered the knife to Bremmer. "Use this."

Lieutenant Bremmer hefted it. "My cousin used to have one just like this."

"The slug," Fargo said.

"Certainly. I only wish we had time to heat some water."

Fargo watched for the Apaches while the lieutenant worked. The others had hold of Jackson's arms and legs to keep him from thrashing.

Jackson tried not to cry out but didn't succeed.

Another trooper removed the shoulder sling from his cartridge pouch and gave it to Jackson to bite on.

"I almost have it," the lieutenant assured him, and twisted the Arkansas toothpick.

Every vein in Private Jackson's face and neck bulged.

Fargo didn't blame him. Bremmer was clumsy about it. But if they didn't get the slug out, the wound might become infected.

And it was a well-known fact that more gunshot victims died of infection than from being shot.

"Almost there," the lieutenant said again.

There was still no sign of the Apaches.

Fargo doubted there would be. Not when the smart thing for the Apaches to do was leave their horses off in the chaparral and attack on foot. They wouldn't raise dust that way, and a man on foot was always harder to hit than a man on horseback.

Private Jackson let out a strangled whine of agony, and slumped.

"He's passed out," a trooper said.

"That's all right." Lieutenant Bremmer proudly held up the bloody piece of lead. "The bullet is out. We can bandage him and go."

Just then the Ovaro raised its head and pricked its ears. It was staring at the north slope.

Fargo's gut told him they had run out of time. He thought he saw movement and jerked the Henry up. Without taking his eyes off the spot, he said, "Bremmer, we have company."

The officer and his men were on their feet in an instant, carbines in hand.

"Get Private Jackson on his horse," Lieutenant Bremmer ordered. "And be quick about it."

"But the bandage?" a man said.

"It will have to wait. Hurry now. If they catch us in a cross fire, we're done for."

Fear lent speed to their efforts. Three of them placed Jackson on his mount and tied him in place as Fargo had done with Major Waxler.

"What are the savages waiting for?" Lieutenant Bremmer whispered. "Why don't they attack?"

As if they had heard him, high on the north slope a swarthy figure popped up from behind a boulder and squeezed off a shot. Evidently that was a signal. Warriors commenced to fire from both sides.

Fargo squeezed off two shots and darted to the Ovaro. It was time to get out of there.

The troopers were working their single-shot carbines as rapidly as they could.

Swinging on, Fargo snapped a shot at an Apache but was sure he missed. "What are you waiting for?" he roared at the soldiers. "Get on your damn horses!" If they didn't, it would be another massacre. He felt a tug at the whangs on his left sleeve and answered in kind.

"To horse! To horse!" Lieutenant Bremmer shouted.

The troopers scrambled to climb on their mounts. A lanky youth was almost on his when he was hit between the shoulder blades. Arching his back, he shrieked and toppled.

Fargo covered them as best he could. Trying to hit an Apache, though, was like trying to hit a ghost. They rarely showed themselves, and when they did they were gone again in the bat of an eye.

Lacking targets, Fargo fired at their gun smoke, hoping to keep them pinned down.

Lieutenant Bremmer and two others were mounted. A last man was trying to climb on but his horse was panicked and shied each time he raised his boot to the stirrup.

"Hurry, man, hurry!" Bremmer bawled.

Reining over, Fargo grabbed the spooked mount's bridle.

"Get on!" he yelled, holding tight as the horse attempted to pull loose.

More war whoops added to the din. Additional warriors had arrived.

The moment the trooper was on, Fargo played a hunch.

The Apaches probably expected them to continue west, not to double back. Not when some of the war party were between the troopers and the fort. But that was exactly what Fargo intended doing. "Stay close!" he bellowed, and reined around.

Lieutenant Bremmer and the surviving soldiers galloped after him.

Fargo was almost clear of the slopes when a warrior hurtled at him, a knife clasped in his hand. Leaping, the Apache slashed at Fargo's leg but Fargo reined aside and kept going.

One of the troopers wasn't as fortunate. The warrior pounced as the soldier raced by and managed to seize the man's leg. Clinging on, the Apache thrust his blade into the trooper's ribs.

Fargo rode for all he was worth, the heat be damned. The soldiers who were left were right behind.

Rifles boomed on the heights but none of them were brought down. The shooting stopped once they were out of range. Apaches weren't ones for wasting ammunition, not when it was so hard for them to come by.

Bremmer shouted Fargo's name but Fargo wasn't about to slow down until he was certain they were out of danger.

They went around a bend, and found a surprise. Not twenty yards from the road were nine Apache mounts, left there when the warriors went ahead on foot.

The Apaches hadn't left a guard but that wasn't surprising. No warrior would pass up a chance to slay blue coats.

Fargo reined over and Lieutenant Bremmer joined him. "Do we scatter them so the devils can't come after us?"

Fargo had a better idea. "We take them with us."

"Steal horses from some of the best horse thieves on the continent?" Lieutenant Bremer laughed. "I like the way you think, mister." He barked orders.

Quickly, the remaining troopers spread out. Whooping and waving their arms, they set the Apache animals into motion.

Fargo wished he could see the looks on their faces when the Apaches found their mounts gone. It wasn't often anyone got the better of them.

After a mile of hard riding, he felt safe in slowing to a walk. "I reckon the worst is over for now."

"I certainly hope so," Lieutenant Bremmer said. "I've lost too many men as it is." He rubbed his chin in thought. "Do you think the ones who attacked us were the same bunch who attacked the paymaster?"

"Most likely," Fargo said.

"Good. They've been getting away with far too much for far too long. It's about time someone beat them at their own bloodthirsty game."

23

"We're not at the fort yet," Fargo said. "We haven't beaten anyone."

"We wouldn't be alive if not for you. Accept credit where credit is due."

"I'd rather have a whiskey," Fargo said.

6

Fort Bowie had been built the year before. It wasn't named after the famous knife fighter Jim Bowie, as some might reckon, but after an officer from California who took part in the ongoing war against the Apaches. The Apaches, in fact, were the reason it existed. The post was intended to safeguard the road through the mountains, in particular a pass and a spring.

Originally the army called it a fort but then changed the name to Camp Bowie because it lacked fortifications. There was no palisade, no permanent barracks or a hospital. The troopers went on calling it Fort Bowie anyway.

The officer in charge was Colonel Chivington. Fargo had never met him but had heard through the scouts' grapevine that Chivington was more than competent.

Fully half the company was preparing to head out when Fargo and Lieutenant Bremmer arrived.

The Apaches' mounts were taken off their hands and driven into a corral, the wounded man was seen to, and Colonel Chivington called Fargo and Bremmer into his office to hear their report. One of the few actual buildings—the men slept in tents—it was Spartan, and small.

Colonel Chivington, after accepting the dispatch from Fargo, listened without saying a word. When they were done, he addressed the lieutenant.

"You did all you could. Don't blame yourself for the loss of your men. These are Apaches we're dealing with. There are no better killers anywhere."

Fargo couldn't have said it better, himself.

"If anyone is to blame, it's that woman," Colonel Chivington continued. "By going off by herself and forcing me to send you after her, she put you and the men with you at risk."

"That she did, sir," Bremmer said bitterly.

"As for you, Mr. Fargo," Chivington said, turning in his chair, "you've been through quite an ordeal. I suggest you rest up while I personally see to the burial detail and the retrieval of government property. I'll have need of you later."

"You will?" Fargo asked. He was under orders to head back once he'd delivered the dispatch.

"We'll discuss it when I return." Chivington rose. "Right now I must attend to the paymaster and his men before the sun and the scavengers take a worse toll."

"I'd like to go with you, sir," Lieutenant Bremmer requested.

"You'll do no such thing," Chivington said as he donned his hat. "You will stay and rest, as well. Captain Andrews will be in charge until I return."

"Yes, sir."

The officers strode out.

Fargo stood. He was sore, hungry and thirsty. Unfortunately, there wasn't a saloon to be had for a hundred miles. There was the mess tent, though, so he could get food, at least.

The camp was bustling, with soldiers hurrying every which way. Those who were leaving were strapping on web belts and seeing to their carbines.

The mess tent was empty, save for the cook and one other person. The cook told him that there wasn't any food to be had at the moment but he was more than welcome to attend the evening meal and help himself. There was coffee, though, and Fargo carried a cup over and said, "Mind some company?"

Geraldine Waxler glanced up as if startled. "Oh. Mr. Fargo. I'm sorry. I was lost in thought."

"Don't apologize," Fargo said, claiming a chair. "You just lost your husband." The fresh hurt in her eyes made him regret the words the moment they were out of his mouth.

"Yes," Geraldine said bleakly. "This has been the worst day of my life. And just when I had started to live again, to hope again."

Fargo didn't pester her with questions. He decided to drink his coffee and drift elsewhere so she could grieve in peace.

"He was a good man, you know," Geraldine said, her face brightening. "The most decent I ever met."

Fargo could have said that a lot of wives felt the same about their husbands. He took a sip, instead.

"I know," Geraldine said. "You think I'm being a typical new bride. But I meant every word. No one knows men better than me, and he was one of the finest."

"I never argue with a lady," Fargo tried to lighten her mood.

"Ah. But there's the rub, as they say," Geraldine replied. "Until I said 'I do,' I was anything but."

Once more Fargo didn't pry. But evidently she wanted to talk about it.

"You must be wondering what I mean."

"No," Fargo said. "I heard about . . ." He stopped.

"My past life?" Geraldine frowned. "Why, of course you have. It must be the talk of the camp, if not the entire army. A woman like me, married to an officer like him."

"They're just jealous."

Geraldine smiled. "What a nice thing to say. But no, we both know the truth. I was a fallen dove when Hank met me, and that's putting it politely."

"I'm fond of doves, myself."

"Most men are, if only for *that*."

"I just like their company," Fargo said. "Doves like to drink and laugh and have a good time, the same as I do."

"That we do," Geraldine said, and caught herself. "Or, rather, I did, before Hank made a decent woman out of me."

"A lot of doves give up the trade," Fargo mentioned. "It's not as if you're stuck at it the rest of your life."

"True, many do. Most because they wear out. They grow old before their time and can't take it anymore. A lot die from too much liquor, or worse. A few, the lucky ones, meet a man who's willing to put their past aside and give them a new life."

Over her shoulder, Fargo saw a couple of troopers come in and draw up short when they spotted her. One said something to the other, both looking as if they'd just tasted something foul.

"That's what Hank did," Geraldine said with wonder in her voice. "He was willing to overlook all that I'd done, the mess I'd made of my life, all the men, everything."

"That happens," Fargo said. The soldiers were whispering, the skinniest gesturing angrily at Geraldine's back.

"Not often. When Hank first told me he loved me and wanted me for his wife, I almost laughed. I thought he was loco. Or drunk."

The soldiers started toward them.

"Hank Waxler gave me the most precious gift there is. Thanks to him, I could start over. I could be a respectable woman again. But do you know what I found out?"

Before Fargo could answer, the pair reached their table. They paid no attention to him. Glaring at Geraldine, the skinny trooper, whose face reminded Fargo of those buzzards he'd seen earlier, poked her in the arm.

"We'd like a word with you, lady."

Geraldine looked up in surprise. "Yes?" she said uncertainly. "Do I know you?"

"No, but we know you," the skinny soldier said.

The other one nodded.

"We know that because of you, a lot of good men were shot to pieces today," the skinny one told her. "Friends of ours."

"They'd still be alive if it weren't for you," the other soldier declared.

"Oh." Geraldine clasped her hands on the table and said contritely, "I'm sorry."

"A little late for that," the skinny soldier said.

"I never meant any harm to come to anyone," Geraldine explained. "I just wanted to see my husband."

"We know about him, too, and what he did," the skinny man said.

"Asking a woman like you to marry him," the other threw in. "What did he use for a brain?"

Geraldine colored and met their glares with her own. "I beg your pardon."

"You heard me," the second man said. He had a hooked nose and a wart on his chin.

The skinny trooper nodded. "Marrying a whore is about as dumb as it gets, and that's no lie."

Fargo had listened to enough. "The lady feels bad enough without you adding to it."

"Who asked you to butt in?" the skinny soldier rejoined.

"Mind your own business, scout," the man with the wart said. "This is between the whore and us."

Fargo went to stand but Geraldine reached across and placed her hand on his wrist.

"Don't. Please. I brought this on myself."

"You didn't do anything wrong," Fargo said.

The skinny soldier jabbed a finger at him. "Like hell she didn't.

She left without permission and the colonel had to send men after her."

"They died on her account," the other said.

Fargo bristled. "They'd already found her and sent her back. They were killed when they went to see about the paymaster and his detail, not over her."

The skinny trooper smirked. "The paymaster was her husband, so it's the same thing."

"That's right." The other man nodded. "And we want this bitch to know that we—"

Fargo heaved up out of his chair. He caught the man with the wart on the jaw with an uppercut that sent him tottering, pivoted, and rammed a fist to the skinny soldier's gut.

"Don't! Please!" Geraldine cried.

The pair hadn't gone down. They were tougher than they looked. Glowering, they raised their fists and the skinny one snarled, "Mister, you shouldn't ought to have done that."

"You take her side, you get what she would if she weren't female," the other trooper said.

"Stop this, you hear?" Geraldine said. "I'll go to the colonel if you don't."

"He left, lady," the skinny trooper said. "And the captain is clear over on the other side of the camp." He glanced at his companion. "How about we pay this bastard back, Hector?"

"Fine by me, Orley," Hector said.

Side by side, they closed in on Fargo.

7

Fargo didn't resort to his Colt. The pair were unarmed. He could pull on them and tell them to make themselves scarce, but that would be letting them off easy.

Orley pumped his bony fists, eager to wade in. "We're going to pound you, mister."

"That we are," Hector agreed.

"Start pounding," Fargo said.

They came in together, both swinging, Orley going for Fargo's face, Hector lower down. Fargo blocked Orley's punch, side-stepped Hector, and unleashed a solid jab to Hector's cheek that jolted Hector onto his bootheels. Geraldine yelled for them to stop but Fargo wasn't about to. Knuckles grazed his jaw and a foot missed his knee. He rammed a right into Orley, whirled and buried his left fist in Hector's gut. Orley retreated, but not Hector. Hector set himself and rained punches; he didn't seem to care what part of Fargo he hit so long as he connected. Fargo countered, weaved, retaliated with a straight-arm to the face that split Hector's cheek.

Suddenly Geraldine was there, pushing between them, her arms thrust out. "Stop this—do you hear me?" she pleaded.

"Go to hell, bitch," Orley snarled, and struck her.

Fargo caught her as she fell. She was doubled over in agony and didn't resist when he pushed her into a chair. Turning back, he felt hot fury course through his veins. He tore into Orley, a one-man hurricane, hammering him, beating down his guard, the thud of his blows like the beat of a drum.

"Help me!" Orley hollered.

Hector came to his friend's aid. He clipped Fargo on the ribs, caught him on the shoulder.

Furious, Fargo brought his right boot down on Hector's instep. Hector cursed and backpedaled, and Fargo went after him. Avoiding a left cross from Orley, he slammed two quick punches into Hector's belly. Hector bent over, putting his face in easy reach of Fargo's knee. Blood spurted, and Hector clutched at his nose. It was doubtful Hector saw the roundhouse right that brought him down.

Orley skipped back, less confident now that he was alone. "Hold on," he said as Fargo came toward him. "Let's call a truce."

"Let's not," Fargo said. He was in no mood to be merciful.

Orley grew frantic. He kicked at Fargo's groin and turned to run but he'd taken only a step when Fargo seized him by the scruff of his collar and hurled him to the ground. Unhurt, Orley sought to scramble to his feet. Fargo met him halfway, with all his weight behind an uppercut.

"You beat them!" Geraldine exclaimed.

Fargo nudged each of the sprawled troopers with his boot to

be sure. Only then did he lean back against a table and take stock of his scrapes and bruises.

"Are you hurt?" Geraldine asked, coming over.

"Nothing worth mentioning," Fargo said. Compared to some fights he'd been in, this had been downright tame.

"We should leave before an officer happens by," Geraldine suggested. "I wouldn't want you to get into trouble on my account."

"I didn't do it for you," Fargo said.

"Sure you didn't." She smiled and touched his cheek. "That was gallant. It was something Hank would have done."

Fargo shrugged and motioned at the unconscious troopers. "Peckerwoods get my dander up."

Geraldine ruefully grinned. "They get mine up, too. This is the sort of thing I've had to put up with ever since Hank married me. But no one has ever been so blatant about it."

Fargo refrained from pointing out that without Hank to stand up for her, she might be in for a lot more of it.

Out of the blue, Geraldine said, "Why don't you come to my quarters? I have something that might cheer you up."

Fargo didn't feel he needed cheering but he went along anyway. Her quarters turned out to be a shack. "This is where they put you up?"

"I've stayed in worse." Geraldine crossed to a dresser. "It's the best they have at the moment." Opening a drawer, she rummaged inside. "I know it's here somewhere. It's Hank's but he never took it with him when he was on duty."

A thought occurred to Fargo. "Maybe I shouldn't be here. Tongues might wag."

"Let them. After what we've been through, you're the closest thing to a friend I have in these parts. If I want to invite you in, I damn well will." Geraldine reached deeper into the drawer, and smiled. "Here it is."

Fargo grinned at the silver flask she held out. "Well, now." Opening it, he sniffed. "Monongahela, by God."

"That suits you?"

Fargo answered by taking a long swig and letting out a contented sigh. "Down to my bones."

Geraldine stepped to a table. "Good. You can keep it." She held up a hand when he began to object. "Hank rarely used it, and there are other things of his I value more."

"I'm obliged," Fargo said.

"I have a favor to ask in return."

"If I can," Fargo said.

"You'll be going after the Apaches who killed him, I take it?"

Fargo hadn't planned to. He'd been sent to deliver the dispatch, nothing more. But now that he thought about it, Colonel Chivington might ask for his help. He was good at tracking. Not that Apaches ever left much sign to follow. "I might be."

"If you do, kill every last one of them. Don't spare a single savage."

Fargo looked at her.

"What?" Geraldine said. "They slaughtered my husband and his men. For that they deserve to be drawn and quartered but I'd settle for a bullet to the brain for each and every one."

"I had no idea you were so bloodthirsty, ma'am," Fargo joked.

Geraldine didn't smile. "Hank meant more to me than anything. He was the one good thing that ever came into my life. He loved me despite what I'd been and done. He deserves justice."

"An eye for an eye," Fargo said.

"Then you do understand." Geraldine's voice became an angry growl. "If I were a man I'd have gone after them myself by now. I wouldn't leave a single one alive."

"We don't know how many took part."

"Find out. And don't rest until you've tracked down each and every one and snuffed out their lives like they snuffed out my husband's."

"Apaches don't die easy," Fargo said.

"You'll have soldiers with you, won't you? I can't imagine that Colonel Chivington will rest until his men have been avenged."

Fargo marveled at how little she knew about the army. The soldiers were there to ensure the road stayed open and to safeguard settlers. Losing a few men now and then came with the job. They weren't in the revenge business.

"You will, won't you?" Geraldine said. "Kill them for me."

"I'll do what I can," was the best Fargo could promise. Taking another swig, he capped the flask and handed it back.

"I said you could keep it."

"It wouldn't feel right." Fargo suspected that she had offered it to him to soften him up so he'd agree to her "favor."

Disappointed, Geraldine replaced the flask in the drawer. "Very well. But you'll find whiskey hard to come by here."

"I can go without when I have to." Fargo touched his hat brim.

"I thank you for the drink, ma'am. See you around." He figured that was the end of it and was reaching for the door when her hand found his.

"You're upset with me, aren't you? I can tell."

"I have things to do," Fargo said.

"Is that the real reason you're leaving so suddenly?"

"Why else?" Fargo smiled, and left. He was glad to be shed of her. While he appreciated how heartbroken she was by the major's death, if she wasn't careful, her thirst for vengeance could get her in trouble.

With so many of the soldiers gone, Fort Bowie lay quiet under the burning sun. The only thing that stirred on the parade ground were puffs of dust fanned by occasional gusts of hot wind. Over in the corral, the horses hung their heads, the Ovaro among them, enduring the heat as best they were able.

Fargo was halfway there when he acquired a second shadow. "Lieutenant Bremmer," he said.

"I'd like a word, if I may."

"I'm listening."

Bremmer scooted around in front of him, forcing him to stop. "I just had an interesting talk with the cook."

"He's making you a bowl of pudding?"

"Cute." The lieutenant shook his head. "He told me he witnessed a fight between you and two of the enlisted men."

"He must have dreamed it," Fargo said.

"Don't patronize me," Bremmer said. "I'd like to know who you fought, and why."

"No."

Lieutenant Bremmer folded his arms. "Need I remind you that you're currently in the employ of the United States Army? Which makes you subject to the same rules and regulations as everyone else."

"Isn't there a rule that scouts can do as they damn well please?"

Bremmer muttered something, then said, "Is it me, or do you seem to have a low regard for authority?"

Fargo started to go around. "No 'seems' about it."

"But you're a scout. You're expected to take orders. I'm ordering you to tell me their names."

"Ask the cook."

"I warn you. I'll report you to Colonel Chivington when he gets back."

Fargo kept going. He hadn't been at the fort much more than

an hour, and already he looked forward to leaving. The list of reasons was as long as his arm: no towns nearby, no saloons, no doves and no card games, the people here were a pain in the backside, and the cook made terrible coffee. As if that wasn't enough, walking toward him were four more reasons.

Orley and Hector and two of their friends.

8

Fargo was in no mood for more of their stupidity. Placing his hand on his Colt, he said, "What the hell do you want?"

Orley smirked and replied, "What do you think?"

"I think you're a jackass."

"I can't wait to bust your teeth," Orley said. "There are enough of us now."

"Not nearly," Fargo said.

Orley tensed to spring but stopped when Hector gripped his arm, whispered and pointed.

Lieutenant Bremmer was coming toward them.

"Damn it all," Orley snarled, and wheeled. "It will have to wait. But we'll be back. Count on it."

The four soldiers turned and hurried off.

Fargo would just as soon have busted a few heads with his Colt. Maybe then they'd leave him be.

"Is everything all right?" Bremmer asked as he came up.

"Why wouldn't it be?"

"Those men looked angry. Were any of them involved in the altercation in the mess tent?"

"They wanted to know if I had any whiskey."

"Did they, now?" Bremmer said. "I'll have a talk with them. They know the colonel strictly forbids drinking on the post." He took off after them.

Fargo went on to the corral and to check on the Ovaro. He had half a mind to saddle up and head out but the stallion could use more rest. For that matter, so could he. Taking his bedroll, he went around to the side of the headquarters building. He spread out his blankets in the shade, lay on his back, and draped his forearm over his eyes to ward off the sun.

Fargo rarely took a midday nap and figured he might not be able to sleep but he was out like a snuffed candle in no time. He didn't sleep long, no more than an hour, judging by the sun.

With nothing to do, he just lay there. He'd give anything for a card game to sit in on. And a bottle. He regretted giving the flask back to Geraldine.

As if she had read his mind, around the corner ambled the lady, herself. She had changed from her pink outfit into a brown blouse and green skirt. A riding outfit, Fargo believed it was called. Instead of a parasol she held a quirt. A large handbag was slung over her shoulder. "There you are. I had to ask nine or ten men before one of them mentioned seeing you asleep over here."

"The hotel was full." Fargo sat up with his back to the wall. Smoothing his hair, he adjusted his hat, waiting for her to say why she had looked him up.

Geraldine dipped to her knees. "We need to talk some more."

"If it's about me killing Apaches for you, I've said all I'm going to."

Geraldine reached into her handbag and held out the flask. "I thought you might like another drink."

"No strings attached this time?" Fargo asked.

Geraldine shook her head. "But I do have a request I'd like to make."

Fargo savored a long swallow, and the burning sensation that spread down to his stomach. "You've got five minutes." That way, he could take his time drinking the rest.

"I've talked to Lieutenant Bremmer. He's of the opinion that after the colonel returns with the bodies, Chivington will want you to try and track the Apaches who slaughtered them."

"I reckon so," Fargo said, and took another swallow.

"Will you go by yourself or lead a patrol?"

"That's not up to me," Fargo answered. The colonel would have the final say. Although, given his druthers, he'd rather go it alone. "Why?"

"Because if it's just you," Geraldine said, "I'd like to go along."

"Be serious."

"I can ride. I can shoot. I'll keep up with you, and I won't complain once."

Fargo shook his head. Here she was again, trying to win him over with the whiskey. Everyone must think he was a drunk. But liking a drink now and then and being booze blind all the time were two different things.

"You're thinking that it's preposterous."

"Lady, you took the words right out of my mouth," Fargo said, and tilted the flask.

"If I were a man you wouldn't say that."

"Is that so?"

"A man wants revenge and it's perfectly fine. A woman wants revenge and she's crazy. Admit it. The only reason you won't take me is because I'm female."

"The reason I won't take you," Fargo said, "is because you'll get yourself killed."

"You can't predict what will happen."

"These are *Apaches* we're talking about," Fargo said. "You never know when they'll pop out of thin air and bury a blade in you."

"Again I say to you, nonsense. They're flesh and blood, like you and me. They die like everybody else."

"You have no notion," Fargo said.

"All I ask is that you consider it."

Fargo decided to be reasonable with her. She deserved that much. "Let's say I take you. And let's say that by some miracle you kill an Apache or two to pay them back for Hank. What then?"

"I haven't thought that far ahead," she admitted.

"Of course you haven't," Fargo rubbed it in. "You haven't thought at all if you think you stand a snowball's chance in hell of making it back alive."

"You're trying to scare me."

"I'm trying to save your idiot hide. And just so you know, I'd do the same if you were a man."

Geraldine pursed her lips, sulking. "I don't see why you're making such a fuss. It's my life, to do with as I want."

"Geraldine," Fargo said in exasperation, "you're not a soldier. You're not a scout or a buffalo hunter or a gambler or a lawman."

"What do they have to do with anything?"

"You've never had to kill," Fargo said. "You're a dove, for God's sake. And you want to tangle with Apaches?"

35

"It doesn't take much to squeeze a trigger."

"Not everybody can. Some folks can't hurt another human being if they tried."

"They don't have cause," Geraldine argued. "I do."

Fargo raised the flask again. He might as well drink as much as he could before she demanded it back. Smacking his lips, he said, "You have cause. I'll grant you that."

"Then you'll do it?"

"No way in hell," Fargo said bluntly.

Those nice lips of hers became a slit. "You're just like every other man I've ever met except for Hank. Pigheaded through and through."

"Listen to you," Fargo said, and laughed. "What do they call that? Something about a pot and a kettle?"

"Poke fun. But I won't be denied. If you refuse to let me help you, I'll go by myself."

"I didn't take you for dumb," Fargo said. The notion of her waging war on the Apaches was plumb ridiculous. "You wouldn't stand a prayer."

"I don't care. Hank was everything to me. He took me out of a life I despised and made me whole again. For six months I was Mrs. Henry Waxler, the proudest woman alive. My heart was his for as long as we lived." Geraldine stopped, her eyes glistening. "And now those redskins have crushed it. They've taken him away from me, and my new life, besides. I'm back where I was before he asked me to marry him. Back to having people look down their noses at me. Back to them thinking I'm no good for nothing at all except one thing."

"I don't think that."

Geraldine blinked, and a tear trickled down her cheek. "I believe you. But you're an exception. Lieutenant Bremmer, and I suspect Colonel Chivington, believe I used my body to entice Hank into marrying me. That I tricked him with my feminine wiles."

"Who cares what they think?"

"I do. I know I shouldn't but I can't help it. And the enlisted men are even worse. They act as if they expect me to go back to my former ways any moment now."

"There's no shortage of idiots," Fargo said.

Despite herself, Geraldine smiled. "Isn't that the truth. Not many men are as understanding as you."

"Understanding, hell," Fargo said. "I like a good time under the sheets as much as anybody."

"But you don't think less of me because of how I used to make my living."

"We've strayed off the trail," Fargo said. "This was about you going after the Apaches."

"Don't think I won't. I have my mind made up. With you or without you, I will avenge my Hank." Rising, Geraldine smoothed her skirt. "Keep the flask. Consider it a gift." Turning, she walked off.

"That's some gal," Fargo said to himself. But he wasn't about to let her get herself killed. He'd talk to the colonel, persuade Chivington to have her escorted to Tucson under guard.

Relaxing, he shook the flask to tell how much whiskey was left. About half, he reckoned. He treated himself to a few more sips, then reluctantly replaced the cap and slid the flask into a pocket. It wouldn't do to be caught with it by Bremmer or some other stickler for regulations.

Standing, Fargo stretched. The nap had done him some good. He felt rested and eager to do something, but what? Bending, he rolled up his blankets, tied one end of the bedroll and then the other.

The scuff of rapid footsteps behind him came too late. He tried to unfurl but a blow to his back pitched him to his hands and knees.

"I've got you now, you son of a bitch."

Fargo looked up.

It was Orley again, and he was holding a knife.

9

Fargo shook his head in disgust. "Some folks never learn."

"You hurt me, mister," Orley spat. "I don't forget a thing like that."

"Where did your pards get to?" Fargo asked, sliding his right hand to his boot.

"The lieutenant put the fear of the stockade into them, but not into me."

Hiking his pants leg, Fargo slid his fingers into his boot and palmed the Arkansas toothpick. "You'll be clapped in irons if Colonel Chivington finds out."

"Who's going to tell him?" Orley motioned. "Look around you. It's just you and me."

Fargo rose to his knees. The camp looked deserted. It was the hottest part of the day, too hot for drilling or most anything else, and few troopers were out and about.

"You just going to kneel there?" Orley said. "Defend yourself. Or did you become yellow all of a sudden?"

"I'm surprised you didn't just stab me," Fargo said as he rose with his right arm, and the toothpick, behind his leg.

"What do you take me for?" Orley said. "I'll give you a chance, like I'd give anybody. This will be fair."

Fargo showed his hand, and his blade. "Yes," he said, "it will."

Undaunted, Orley grinned. "If you're thinking to scare me, think again. There's something you don't know."

"What would that be?"

"I may not look like much but I'm a hellion with a knife."

"Prove it."

Orley did. He leaped to the attack, flashing his knife high and low and slashing from side to side.

It was all Fargo could do not to be cut. Parrying, evading, he was forced to give way. He retreated a couple of steps, and planted himself. Orley wasn't all brag; he truly was good. But so was Fargo.

Jerking his arm away to avoid having his wrist opened, Fargo cut Orley and drew blood.

Now it was Orley who took a step back. He glanced at the red drops, and swore. "You're quick, scout. Mighty quick. But it won't help."

"And you talk too much."

Orley raised his hand to his mouth and licked his knuckles. Smirking, he spat blood at Fargo's face but Fargo got his hand up.

Tucking at the knees, Orley came at him again. "No more talk. We end this."

Fargo was glad to oblige. He feinted, twisted, lunged. Orley countered, shifted, drove his knife at Fargo's neck. Cold steel rang on cold steel and they parted.

Orley growled in frustration. "So far you've been lucky."

38

"Thought you were done talking," Fargo taunted. "Or are you building up your nerve?"

"I'll show you nerve," Orley said.

Their knives became streaks. This time it was Fargo who felt a sharp sting and looked down to see scarlet drops on his hand.

"Not so tough, are you?" Orley gloated.

Fargo stabbed at Orley's throat, expecting to drive the trooper back a couple of steps, but Orley ducked and drove the tip of his blade at Fargo's gut. Fargo barely countered in time. Swiveling, he retaliated with a lightning flick of his wrist and felt his blade slice deep into Orley's upper arm. Bleating in pain, Orley skipped away, or tried to. With a swift bound, Fargo kicked Orley in the shin. Momentarily off balance, Orley glued his gaze to the Arkansas toothpick. It was doubtful Orley saw Fargo's left fist but Orley certainly felt the full force on his chin. Orley's legs buckled, and Fargo slugged him again. He didn't hold back.

The trooper crumpled.

Fargo took a few deep breaths. He had half a mind to report Orley to Lieutenant Bremmer, but no, this was personal. Wiping the toothpick on Orley's shirt, he replaced it in his ankle sheath, reclaimed his bedroll, and left the shade of the building for the inferno of the sun.

Fargo came to a decision. He was tired of the nonsense at Fort Bowie. He'd go find Colonel Chivington, find out if the colonel did indeed want him to go after the Apaches, and if not, light a shuck.

No one saw him off. Lieutenant Bremmer was probably in a tent somewhere. Geraldine was upset because he wouldn't let her get herself killed. The few enlisted men out and about paid him no mind whatsoever.

"Sorry, big fella," Fargo said as he gigged the Ovaro and pulled his hat brim low against the harsh glare.

The good thing about Arizona in the summer was that the heat was a dry heat. It wasn't like, say, Louisiana, where the humidity caused a man to sweat buckets. Fargo sweated, to be sure, but his buckskins didn't become so wet they clung to him.

He stayed alert for Apaches but suspected the war party had melted into the wilderness. Colonel Chivington had half the command with him. Granted, a lot of the troopers were green behind the ears, but they were all well armed, and Apaches never took risks they didn't need to.

Wildlife was scarce. Fargo saw a coyote slinking off. He saw

39

his old friend, the hawk, pinwheeling on high. He glimpsed the backside of a jackrabbit.

By now, Fargo figured, the colonel had reached the ambush site. It wouldn't take the soldiers long to collect the bodies and right the overturned wagon. They may already be on their way back.

But Fargo saw no sign of them. Not at the midway point. Not at the spot where the warriors had sprung up out of the ground to attack Lieutenant Bremmer and his men. It wasn't until he had less than a quarter of a mile to go that the thud of hooves and the rattle of a wagon brought him to a stop.

Fargo didn't have long to wait before the point riders came around a bend, and after them the paymaster's wagon and the main column.

Colonel Chivington, to Fargo's surprise, was up on the seat next to a corporal handling the team. The colonel raised an arm and bellowed, and presently the wagon came to a stop alongside the Ovaro.

"Mr. Fargo. This is a surprise. I expected to find you at Camp Bowie."

"Lieutenant Bremmer said you might want me to track down the Apaches who attacked the paymaster."

"I do, indeed," Chivington said. "I intended to tell you when we got back."

"Why wait?" Fargo said, and raised his reins.

"Just a moment," Chivington said. "You shouldn't go alone. I'll send half a dozen men along."

"They'd only slow me," Fargo said.

"They're good men. They'll do their best to keep up."

"And make a lot more noise than I would by myself. The Apaches will know we're coming from a mile off. We'll never catch them."

The colonel removed his hat, mopped his brow with his sleeve, and put the hat back on. "You're a stubborn cuss."

"And proud of it."

Chivington chuckled. "Very well. Common sense says you're making a mistake but General Owen speaks highly of your abilities. He confided in me once that he thinks you're the best scout the army has."

"He exaggerated," Fargo said. "He likes that I bring him a bottle now and then."

"Get going before I change my mind. And keep your eyes peeled. Good scouts are hard to come by."

Fargo waited until the last of the troopers went past before he rode on. At last he was on his own. He could set his own pace, go wherever the trail led him.

The bleak heights that loomed over the ambush site were littered with talus. Rather than try to climb them and risk breaking the stallion's leg, Fargo circled around. At the crest he cast about for sign, not really expecting to find any.

He found a lot.

There were tracks coming from below. Tracks where the ambushers had spread out. Tracks where they'd descended partway to the road to prepare their ambush. Tracks where they had climbed back up and rushed to their horses.

So many tracks, Fargo should be happy. Following them would be as easy as anything.

"This just can't be." Dismounting, Fargo examined one set of footprints and then another. He studied the heel marks and shapes of the soles. He noted the width of the strides the ambushers took.

There could be no mistake but Fargo refused to believe the evidence of his own eyes. He'd never come across anything like it.

He had been wrong.

The colonel had been wrong.

Everyone had been wrong.

The hoofprints confirmed what the footprints told him. He summed it up with a shake of his head and an "I'll be damned."

Some of the hoofprints were deeper leaving than they had been coming. The pack animals, he reckoned, laden with the heavy money bags.

The sun was sinking when Fargo began his pursuit. They had a good lead but they couldn't push too hard or their packhorses would give out. He had high hopes of overtaking them by daylight, or not long after.

"Won't they be surprised?" Fargo said to the Ovaro, and laughed.

He went over in his head what he had learned. There had been five of them. Cartridges he'd found revealed that all five had repeaters. Probably some of the newest models. Henrys, maybe, like his own. The tracks hinted that one was heavyset but the rest were of middling height and build.

The thing that had startled him, the thing that amazed him, the thing he couldn't quite believe, was that the five cold-blooded killers who had ambushed the paymaster's detail and wiped the soldiers out—were women.

10

Women didn't dress like men. Their shoes, in particular, made it easy to tell a man's footprint from a woman's. The heels were narrower. The soles often came to a tip where the men's were more rounded. The arch was nearly always higher.

Women didn't walk like men, either. Their gait was different. A lot of it had to do with the fact that women, by and large, had wider hips, and because women put more weight on the front of their feet for better balance.

So there was no chance Fargo was mistaken. The party that attacked the paymaster weren't Apaches, as he'd imagined.

The warriors he'd seen and tangled with must have heard the shots and come to investigate. But they hadn't taken part in the robbery.

Fargo couldn't get over it. Female outlaws were as rare as hen's teeth. He could count the number he'd run across in his travels on one hand. An entire gang of lady outlaws was unheard of.

It raised a host of questions. Who were they? Where were they from? Where had they learned to ride and shoot? A lot of women could ride but few women had much experience with firearms. Most went from cradle to grave without touching one.

Their audacity astounded him. And in Apache territory, no less. Most whites were too afraid of Apaches to venture far from civilization, yet the five women were traipsing around the heart of Apache country unfazed.

They had nine horses, all told. Five for the women and four packhorses to carry the money and whatever grub and supplies they'd brought along.

The repeaters, the extra horses. If nothing else, they were organized. Their ambush had been well thought out. That alone was food for thought.

At the present the women were heading northwest. Eventually

42

they'd reach Tucson. Or maybe they were pushing for Phoenix. It was too early to tell.

Sunset painted the sky with vivid colors that faded to the gray of twilight, and the gray in turn darkened to the blue-black of night. A host of stars sparkled, the sky so clear that it lent the illusion Fargo could reach up and touch them.

He didn't stop. He figured that the women would make camp, and their campfire would give them away.

An hour went by and then two, and the only lights were the stars.

Fargo frowned. Either the women hadn't stopped or they were savvy enough to hide their fire. If that was the case, he might pass them without knowing it.

"Damn," Fargo grumbled. As much as he didn't want to, he drew rein. He couldn't chance losing their sign. If he did, he could spend half a day or more finding it again.

Reluctantly, he reined into a wash and dismounted. He didn't bother with a fire. Stripping the Ovaro, he gave the stallion some water from his canteen, using his hat to hold it, and made himself comfortable. A few pieces of jerky sufficed for his supper. He was on the verge of dozing off when a faint clink reached his ears. The sound a hoof might make on rock.

Instantly, Fargo was on his feet. Drawing his Colt, he climbed to the top of the wash. He listened but the sound wasn't repeated. The only thing he heard were the distant yips of a coyote.

Fargo returned to his blankets. He couldn't stay up all night. He needed to be raring to go at daybreak. Lying back down, he stared at the heavens until his eyelids grew too heavy to keep them open.

The next Fargo knew, the Ovaro nickered. He was up in a crouch before he was fully awake. He saw that the stallion's head was up, ears pricked to the south. Flattening, he crawled up the wash, removed his hat, and peered over the rim.

The sky to the east had brightened. Dawn wasn't far off. He could make out some mesquite and a manzanita or two, as well as some shindagger agave, as it was called. But nothing moved.

Jamming his hat on, Fargo slid back down. He skipped breakfast. He didn't even make coffee.

In less than ten minutes he was in the saddle. It was light enough that he could take up following the tracks. Only there weren't any.

He'd lost them. The night before, during those two hours he'd ridden in the dark, he'd drifted off their trail.

Fargo swore. He should have stopped sooner. He roved in a circle, and when he didn't find anything, rode in a wider one. He began to think he'd lost them for good when, on his fourth sweep, he found their tracks.

With a sigh of relief, Fargo resumed his hunt. In the cool of early morning he trotted for over a mile to make up for lost time.

It was apparent the women hadn't stopped for the night. They knew the army would be after them.

Fargo admired their grit. He was impressed even more by the fact that they had stuck to their beeline to the northwest. That meant they had navigated by the stars. A feat not even a lot of men could do.

"Well done, ladies," he said in appreciation, and smiled.

The coolness gave way to the rising heat of the new day. Other than a lizard and later a rattlesnake, there were no signs of life.

Along about noon a feeling came over him, as it sometimes did when his instincts were trying to warn him of something. Drawing rein, he turned in the saddle.

Someone was trailing him.

Fargo didn't see anyone but he'd learned long ago not to argue with his gut. It nearly always proved to be right.

Up ahead were some boulders, high enough to conceal the Ovaro. Climbing down, he slid the Henry from the scabbard, moved to where he could watch his back trail, and sat with his back to one of the boulders with the rifle across his lap. He'd give it half an hour. That was all he could spare. If no one showed, he'd head out again.

Fargo wondered if Apaches had picked up his scent. If so, he'd have to shake them before he could go after the women.

The temperature was pushing one hundred. A heat haze shimmered, distorting objects far off.

It wasn't long before Fargo's precaution was rewarded. The rider was a stick, the horse a blob. Gradually, Fargo saw them more clearly. A jolt of recognition made him blurt, "Son of a bitch." He supposed he shouldn't be surprised but he was.

Some people never listened. They were too pigheaded for their own good.

He stayed by the boulder.

The rider was so intent on the tracks that she didn't look up until she was almost on top of him. "You!" she declared, bringing her sorrel to a halt.

"Fancy seeing you here," Fargo said.

Geraldine Waxler wore the same outfit as the day before, the brown blouse and green riding skirt with black boots that came nearly to her knees. She also had a revolver strapped around her waist, and a rifle butt jutted from her saddle scabbard. "Damn," she said.

Fargo stood and cradled the Henry.

"How did you know I was following you?"

Fargo didn't answer.

"I thought I was being careful," Geraldine said. "I thought I stayed far enough back that you wouldn't."

Fargo stared.

"Cat got your tongue? Say something, will you? Don't just stand there glaring."

"You shouldn't have come after me."

Geraldine's face twisted with resentment. "You have no right to tell me what I can and can't do. No one does."

"Does Colonel Chivington know you're here?"

"As if I'd let him in on my plans," Geraldine said. "Even if I'd told him I intended to go after the killers myself, I doubt he'd have cared. He looks down his nose at me the same as most of the enlisted men. To him I'm nothing but a lowly whore."

"So you snuck off by your lonesome."

"I didn't have to sneak. After I found out you had gone, I saddled my horse and left."

"You were hoping I'd lead you to them," Fargo guessed, "so you can have your revenge."

"I had notions along those lines, yes," Geraldine admitted. "But I don't really need you." She nodded at the prints. "This many tracks, I can follow them on my on."

"And when you catch up to them?"

"What do you think? I won't let you stop me," Geraldine said. "I've come this far, I'll see it through." She put her hand on her revolver. "If you try, I'll do whatever it takes."

"You'd shoot me?"

"I don't know," Geraldine said. "I've never shot anyone. But you know what Hank meant to me. If I have to, yes, I believe I could."

"And the Apaches?"

"What about them? They don't scare you. Why should they scare me?"

"I've fought them before. You haven't."

"I don't care. They killed my husband and I will by God kill them or die trying."

Fargo realized she didn't know the truth yet. She must not have paid much attention to the footprints. He debated enlightening her and decided not to. "You have me over a barrel," he said.

"If I do it's news to me."

"I can't afford the time it would take to return you to Fort Bowie."

"I wouldn't let you anyway."

"And I can't tie you over your saddle and give your horse a smack on the rump in the hope it will find its way back by itself."

"You would do that if the fort were closer?"

"The way I see it," Fargo concluded, "is that the only thing I can do is take you with me."

Grinning, Geraldine took her hand off her revolver. "I didn't expect you to be so reasonable."

"I didn't reckon you would," Fargo said dryly.

"But remember what I said. If this is some kind of trick, if you try to stop me, I'll do whatever I must to thwart you."

"Just so you don't try to stab me in the back when I'm not looking," Fargo said.

Geraldine's grin widened. "You never know," she said.

11

Fargo had accepted the inevitable. There was no way in hell he could stop Geraldine from going after her husband's killers short of hitting her over the head and hog-tying her, and even then, once she freed herself she'd be right back at it.

The smart thing, he reckoned, was to keep her close so he could keep an eye on her and maybe keep her safe.

They had been on the go for over an hour, and he still hadn't revealed that the bushwhackers were women. There was no predicting how she'd react. She was smart enough to know that caution was called for when tangling with Apaches. But other women? She might charge off to confront them.

Just then Geraldine cleared her throat. "I have a question."

Fargo grunted.

"I'm not a tracker. I can't read sign like you do." Geraldine motioned at the tracks they were following. "But I'm not stupid, either. And unless I'm badly mistaken, the horses we're following are all shod."

"They are," Fargo said.

Geraldine's brow knit. "Everyone knows Indians don't ride shod horses. Or do they?"

"They don't, unless it's one they've stolen from a white."

"Then"—Geraldine regarded the tracks with puzzlement—"that means Apaches weren't to blame."

"It does."

"God in heaven," Geraldine exclaimed. "Are you telling me the bastards who murdered my husband are white?"

"It would appear so," was all the further Fargo would commit himself.

"Outlaws!" Geraldine declared. "Here I thought it was savages and it's outlaws." She smacked her leg in anger. "How many? You must be able to tell, as good as folks say you are."

"Five," Fargo said.

"That's all? Five men wiped out my husband and all those soldiers?"

"The outlaws had rifles and they were well hid." Fargo imagined that most of the troopers fell at the first volley.

"White men!" Geraldine said. "This changes everything."

"White or red, it makes no difference."

"Not to you maybe. You're used to fighting Indians, as you keep pointing out. I'm not, and I don't mind confessing I was worried about what would happen when I caught up to them." Geraldine squared her shoulders. "Not now. Whites don't scare me a lick. I can hold my own with them."

"You're awful confident all of a sudden."

"Why shouldn't I be? When it comes to killing, whites can't hold a candle to Apaches."

She had him there, Fargo mused. But it wouldn't do for her to become too cocky. "It's not as if they'll give up without a fight."

"I don't want them to," Geraldine said. "Let them do their worst. I aim to kill every last one of the sons of bitches."

On that note she fell silent.

Fargo devoted himself to the sign, and to constantly scanning the surrounding countryside.

In time the tracks led up an incline to a ridge. There, the outlaws had stopped, no doubt to do some scanning of their own. Several had climbed down and stretched their legs.

Fargo didn't want Geraldine to get a good look at the footprints. Barely slowing, he pushed on.

"It looks as if they rested a bit," Geraldine remarked. "I wouldn't mind stopping for a while, myself."

"You're more than welcome to," Fargo said, hoping she wouldn't.

"But you're not going to? And why is that?"

"They're far enough ahead as it is."

Geraldine eyed him suspiciously. "Is that the real reason you won't mind if I stop? Or is it because you think you can lose me? Maybe wipe out the tracks so I can't follow?"

"I wouldn't do that to you."

"Aren't you noble all of a sudden?" Geraldine said sarcastically. "Well, you can think again. I'm not stopping if you're not. You won't get rid of me that easy."

"You saw right through me," Fargo said dryly.

"I knew it. You only agreed to let me come because you're hoping to throw me off the scent somehow. Admit it."

"Anyone ever tell you how pretty you are when you're mad?"

"Hank used to."

She fell silent again.

Fargo was glad. He couldn't afford to be distracted.

As the afternoon waned, he found himself marveling at the stamina of those he was after. The women hadn't slept a wink all night. Their only rest was that brief spell on the ridge. Yet they showed no sign of stopping anytime soon.

They'd have to stop for the night, though. They couldn't go two whole days without sleep.

The thought made Fargo yawn. He figured the women would stop early, but although he watched the horizon with eagle eyes as the sun transformed into a red orb, he never once spotted the telltale smoke from a campfire.

"I have another question," Geraldine unexpectedly piped up.

"I can't wait," Fargo said.

"Be nice. I've been nice to you, haven't I?" Without waiting for an answer, Geraldine asked, "What do you plan to do once we overtake them? I know what *I* want to do. But you haven't said whether you aim to take them alive or do what should be done."

When he'd first set out, Fargo had taken it for granted the killers were Apaches. He'd had no compunction at all about doing to them as they'd done to the troopers. But now things were different.

"Well?" Geraldine prodded when he didn't say anything.

"Taking them alive would be best," Fargo said. As a general rule, he didn't shoot women if he could help it.

"Why go to all that bother? So what if they're white? They deserve a bullet to the brain. Nothing less."

"I'm not a judge or a jury," Fargo said.

"So? We walk up to them and do it. It's as simple as that."

"Are you fixing to gun them in their bedrolls?" Fargo asked, only partly in jest.

"If it comes to that," Geraldine said. "Weren't you the one who told me I shouldn't take chances?"

"Yes, but—"

Geraldine held up a hand. "I don't want to hear it. You can't say one thing one minute and change your mind later on. When we catch up, we'll take them in their sleep and exterminate them."

"You're not to lift a finger against them without my say-so."

"The hell you say," Geraldine said. "I'll do as I please, thank you very much."

Fargo smothered an urge to climb down, find a suitable rock and bean her with it.

"Yes, sir," Geraldine said, more to herself than to him. "By this time tomorrow it should be over."

Fargo still didn't see any smoke. If he didn't spot some soon, he'd stop. He'd learned his lesson the night before.

"Have you clammed up on me again?" Geraldine asked indignantly. "I swear, you're the most contrary man I've ever set eyes on."

Fargo was about to tell her that she wasn't easy to get along with, either, when fifty yards out or so, he saw a gleam of light. It was there and it was gone. If he'd blinked, he'd have missed it.

The last of the sunlight . . . reflecting off a gun barrel.

Fargo hurled himself from his saddle. He heard the boom of a shot as his arms went around Geraldine. She squawked in surprise, and they tumbled. Fargo tried to twist in midair so he would bear the worst of it but they thudded hard on their sides.

Pain flared, and Fargo gritted his teeth and rolled, taking

49

Geraldine with him. She was so confused she resisted. The crash of a second shot brought her head up.

"Someone is shooting at us!"

None too gently, Fargo hauled her into some mesquite. "Keep your voice, and your head, down." Wishing he had the Henry, he drew his Colt.

Geraldine drew her own revolver, so awkwardly it was apparent she'd never used it. "Who's doing the shooting? The outlaws? Or Apaches?"

"Stand up and ask them."

"You just told me to keep my head down," Geraldine said, and blinked. "Oh. I get it."

Fargo eased higher to try to see over the mesquite. The blast of the rifle disabused him; he swore he heard the slug whistle past his ear.

"Whoever it is," Geraldine said, "they're not a very good shot."

A whinny filled Fargo with fresh worry. The Ovaro and her sorrel had stopped, and it might occur to the shooter to kill their mounts and strand them on foot.

"What do we do?" Geraldine whispered.

"*We* do nothing," Fargo said. "You stay put while I get closer." To forestall another argument, he crawled off. A boulder offered some protection. From there he snaked into a gully. It was shallow but it pointed in the right direction.

This was what came from letting Geraldine come along, Fargo chided himself. He'd been spatting with her instead of staying alert, and now look.

Putting her from his mind for the time being, Fargo concentrated on finding the shooter. There appeared to be only one. Or was it a trick, and others were lying in wait for him to show himself?

The snap of a twig caused him to freeze. It came from his left.

As quietly as possible, Fargo crawled to the top of the gully. High grass and scrub brush were all around him. Extending the Colt, he thumbed back the hammer.

A stone's throw away, grass parted and out of it poked a rifle barrel.

The shooter had seen him.

12

Fargo threw himself at the bottom of the gully just as the rifle boomed. He rolled, pebbles clattering under him. Quickly rising to his knees in case the shooter rushed him, he waited with every nerve jangling.

No one appeared.

Keeping low, Fargo glided up the gully. When he had gone far enough to consider it safe, he moved to the top again.

The rifle barrel was gone.

Tensing, Fargo raced for the cover. He was halfway there when a rifle spanged. It felt as if his hat was slapped but it stayed on his head and in a few more bounds he was prone in the grass.

Time for some cat and mouse, Fargo told himself. Crawling away from the shooter, he circled wide to come up on the assassin from behind.

The rifle banged, and he hugged the ground, thinking he was the target. But, no. A revolver answered from over near the horses. It was Geraldine. She hadn't stayed put as he'd told her to.

The shooter fired again.

Throwing caution aside, Fargo rose. The shots would drown out whatever sounds he made. He spied a crouched form partially hidden by mesquite and flew toward it.

Geraldine blasted twice with her six-gun.

The shooter ducked, then straightened, craning to try to see Geraldine. Fargo glimpsed a floppy brown hat and a man's shirt. Streaking around bush, he hollered, "Hey!"

The shooter spun. A pair of green eyes widened in alarm.

Fargo slammed into her with his shoulder. The impact sprawled her on her back and her rifle, a Spencer, tumbled from her hands. Not missing a beat, she grabbed for a Smith & Wesson at her waist, worn for a cross draw. She was quicker than he'd have thought but not quite quick enough. He arced the Henry at her head. At the thud, she collapsed.

"Got you," Fargo said. He relieved her of the Smith & Wesson and patted her clothes. There were no other weapons.

Fargo was about to yell to Geraldine when her revolver cracked. The bullet chipped mesquite not an inch away. Cupping a hand to his mouth, he bellowed, "Hold your damn fire!"

"Skye? Is that you?"

"Who the hell else?"

"Sorry. I couldn't tell what was going on over there."

Fargo swore under his breath. He was in as much danger from his "partner" as from the outlaws. "Bring the horses and get my rope."

While he waited, he studied his prisoner. She looked to be in her mid- to late thirties. Brown hair hung from under her hat, and she had a dimple on her chin. She wore men's clothes, except for her footwear. Popular with the ladies, they were called "riding shoes."

Geraldine arrived out of breath, leading the Ovaro and her sorrel. She took his rope from his saddle, handed it to him, and squatted. "Let's have a look at the—" She stopped in surprise. "It's a woman!"

Fargo drew his toothpick to cut the rope. "The first of many surprises to come, I reckon."

"*She's* one of the outlaws?"

"Unless she mistook us for deer." Fargo set to binding the woman's wrists.

"I never heard of a female outlaw. Who do you think she is?"

"I left my crystal ball in my other saddlebags," Fargo said.

"Want me to wake her?"

"Not yet."

Geraldine shook her head in amazement. "This defies belief. Why did the other outlaws ride off and leave her?"

"There you ago again," Fargo looped rope around the woman's ankles. Better safe than kicked where it hurt most.

"Look at her face," Geraldine said.

"What about it?"

"She has carmine on her lips. And blue eye shadow. What kind of outlaw gussies up like that?"

"She must want to look pretty when they put her on trial." Fargo motioned. "Fetch my canteen."

"Why am I doing all the work? Can't you do it yourself?" Geraldine stepped to the Ovaro. "Or is it that you're mad at me for almost shooting you and this is your way of getting back at me?" She brought the canteen back. "Here."

Fargo took a swallow. The water was warm but relieved his dry throat. He poured some into his other hand and lightly splashed it on the woman with the red lips. "Rise and shine, lady."

The shooter moaned and muttered but her eyes didn't open.

Fargo wet his palm and pressed it to her forehead and her cheeks. "If you're playing possum, I'll gag you and drag you along behind us."

The woman opened her eyes. Given that she had been hit over the head and tied up, she was remarkably calm. She looked Fargo up and down, then did the same with Geraldine.

"Who are you?" Geraldine asked.

Those red lips curled in a cattish smile. "Wouldn't you like to know, dearie?"

"You'll tell us sooner or later," Geraldine said. "You'll tell us who you are and how you're involved with the payroll robbery and who the men are you're riding with."

"Men?" the woman said, and laughed.

"Their names," Geraldine said. "All of them."

"You silly, silly goose," the woman said. "The truth isn't what you think it is."

Geraldine glanced at Fargo. "What is she talking about?"

"Why ask him?" the woman said. "He doesn't know, either." She wriggled and rose onto her elbows. "So what now? You take me to Fort Bowie and turn me in?"

"I'd just as soon shoot you," Geraldine said, "but I want information first."

"You're no killer," the woman said. "You're a whore who got lucky, is all."

"I beg your pardon?"

"You heard me," the woman said. "That major fell in love with you and proposed. You saw your chance to get off the line and jumped at it. Now that he's dead, what will you do? Go back to spreading your legs for money?"

Geraldine struck her. It happened so fast, there was nothing Fargo could do. She hit the woman flush on the cheek hard enough to rock her head. "You miserable bitch!" Geraldine raised her fist to hit the woman again.

Lunging, Fargo grabbed her wrist. "No."

"You heard her," Geraldine said, trying to wrest free. "She can't talk to me like that."

The woman regarded Geraldine with amusement more than anything else. "Feel better now?"

"How did you know that about me?" Geraldine said. "I've never met you before."

"We know all about you," the woman said. "About your husband, too. Former husband, I should say."

This time Fargo was ready when Geraldine cocked her arm. "I told you no," he said, clamping hard on her forearm.

"What's going on here?" Geraldine said. "How does she know so much about me?"

"Hell, dearie," the woman said, "that was nothing. You were born and raised in Ohio. Married your first husband out of love but he was a no-account and left you."

"How in the world?" Geraldine marveled.

"You had a child to feed and needed work, but you weren't good at much except sewin' and lyin' on your back. One thing led to another and you wound up at a sportin' house in Denver. You weren't there long when your little girl died. Fever, wasn't it?"

Geraldine gaped.

"I almost feel sorry for you," the woman said. "Lost one of my own about ten years ago, and I've never been the same. As for you, you were crushed. You drifted and ended up in Tucson, where you met your darlin' major. And here you are."

"Hank Waxler was the best man who ever lived . . ." Geraldine said.

"Spare me," the woman scoffed. "There's no such thing as a good man. They're all as worthless as teats on a bull."

"I don't reckon I've ever been called a teat before," Fargo said.

"By your buckskins and how you tracked us, I take you for a scout," the woman guessed.

"So you don't know everything."

"Just about her," the woman said, nodding at Geraldine.

"How?" Geraldine asked.

"You were the key, dearie."

"The what?"

The woman smiled and shook her head. "No, you don't. I've talked too much as it is."

"Not nearly," Fargo said, but he would let it go for now. "Where's your horse?"

"Would you believe I walked the whole way?"

Fargo turned to Geraldine. "Can I trust you not to beat her senseless while I go find it?"

"You ask a lot," Geraldine said. "I don't like her playing with us. She was one of those as killed my Hank. I want her spitting blood."

"Can I trust you?"

"You have my word," Geraldine said reluctantly.

Fargo stood. "I suspect her horse is over that ridge, yonder. I shouldn't be long." He turned, but took only a single step.

Someone else was already on the ridge, looking down at them. An Apache.

13

The warrior was astride a bay with a saddle. He was holding a rifle with the stock resting on his thigh and made no attempt to use it.

"That's my horse!" the woman with the red lips exclaimed. "That redskin is stealing it!"

Showing no concern whatsoever, the Apache reined around and rode down the far side.

"Don't just stand there, damn you," the woman railed at Fargo. "Go after him. Bring my horse back."

"It's not my animal," Fargo said. The warrior plainly had no desire to tangle with them and was leaving. He'd like to leave it that way.

Growling deep in her throat, the woman managed to sit up. "Then cut me free so I can try to stop him. My saddlebags are on that horse. Nearly everything I own, except the clothes and what-not I left in—" She abruptly stopped.

"Left where?" Geraldine asked.

The woman shook her head. "I'm not saying another word."

Geraldine turned to Fargo. "What do we do with her? We only have our two horses."

"I say we leave her here," Fargo said. "She'd slow us down, and we have the rest of the outlaws to catch."

"Fine by me," Geraldine said. "I have no sympathy for her whatsoever. For all I know, she might have been the one who shot my Hank."

"You'd leaved me trussed up and helpless?" the woman said in disbelief.

"There are plenty of rocks around," Fargo said.

"And what? I find one with an edge and cut myself free? What then? I have no water, no guns."

"Poor you," Geraldine said. She stood and stepped to her sorrel and reached for the saddle horn. "I hope you die from thirst. They say it takes a good long while and hurts like hell."

"Sister, please," the woman said.

Bristling in fury, Geraldine jabbed a finger at her. "I'm not your damn sister. I'm a woman you deprived of the man she loved, and I'll hate you until my dying day."

"You should be on our side, not theirs," the woman said.

"Whose?" Geraldine snapped. "You make no damn sense." She hooked her foot in the stirrup and pulled herself up. "Come on, Skye. Let's leave her like you said."

Fargo stepped to the Ovaro and hiked his leg to climb on.

"Wait!" the woman cried. "Please." She gazed anxiously about and licked her red lips. "I wouldn't last three days on my own. If the sun doesn't fry me, something else will do me in."

Fargo faced her and folded his arms. "You want us to take you with us?"

"How many times do I have to say it?" she replied.

"Your name."

"I can't."

Fargo shrugged and turned back to the Ovaro. "When you're so thirsty you'll drink you own blood, it will be too late."

"Damn you," the woman spat. "All right. Everyone calls me Ruby on account of I like a lot of carmine on my lips. Will that do?"

"It's not your real name," Geraldine said.

"You stay out of this," Ruby said. "It's between the scout and me."

She focused on Fargo. "If you take me, I'll make it worth your while."

"Oh, brother," Geraldine said. "You didn't just offer your body to him, did you?"

"Why not?" Ruby said. "He can't tell by these clothes but I'm

56

easy on the eyes. And I can do things with him that no woman has ever done."

"That would take some doing," Fargo said.

"Will you or won't you?" the woman asked. "I'll do as you tell me and not make trouble."

"You expect us to trust you?" Geraldine said.

"I wasn't talking to you." Ruby held out her bound wrists to Fargo. "What do you say, mister? Do right by me and I swear to God I'll do right by you."

"You're not falling for her lies, are you?" Geraldine said.

"We take her," Fargo said.

"She's not riding with me."

"Didn't expect her to." Walking over, Fargo hunkered, scooped Ruby into his arms, and carried her to the Ovaro.

"My, oh my," Ruby teased. "Aren't you the bundle of muscle."

Fargo smiled and without breaking stride swung her up and over the Ovaro—belly down. Ruby squawked and tried to wriggle off, but he held her fast and climbed on behind her. Raising the reins, he said, "Comfortable?"

"Damn you, not like this."

"You wanted to come." Fargo clucked to the stallion.

"Let me ride double. I promise to behave."

"It's this or I dump you in the dirt."

Geraldine laughed. "Now you're talking."

Ruby indulged in a string of oaths. She squirmed and kicked but Fargo held her down with ease.

"The mouth on that hussy," Geraldine said.

Ruby finally subsided. Bending her neck to see Fargo, she said, "I'm not above begging if that's what it takes."

"One more word, one more kick, and I leave you," Fargo said.

That quieted her for about an hour.

The heat was blistering. Fargo imagined it was worse for Ruby, what with the hot saddle under her and the sun broiling her back. When she muttered something, he smacked her on her fanny and said, "I didn't catch that."

"I was saying how I'd like to slit your throat," Ruby said.

"Killed a lot of folks, have you?"

"No, not really." Ruby looked up at him. "Those soldiers were the first I've ever killed, and it wasn't like I thought it would be. I didn't feel excited or anything. Mostly I felt sort of sad for them, after."

"You almost shot me."

"It wasn't as if I wanted to. I drew the short piece of grass."

"How's that again?"

"We knew you were after us," Ruby said. "She has a spyglass, and she spotted you this morning. She broke a blade of grass and held the pieces in her hand, and whoever drew the short piece was to wait for you and do you in."

"Who is this 'she' you keep mentioning?"

"Can't," Ruby said. "She'd skin me alive if she found out I told you."

"She's not like you, I take it?" Fargo fished. "She doesn't mind killing."

"Oh, Lordy, no. I never suspected, all those months we worked together, but she's as mean as they come when she has to be. She'll kill anyone, anytime. She even killed the man we bought the repeaters from. Up and bashed him over the head with a rock and stood there laughing as his brains oozed out."

"Why him?" Fargo was curious.

"She didn't trust him. She got it into her head that he might turn us in for any reward that's offered, so she did him in, then and there."

"Can't wait to meet the lady," Fargo said.

"You'd better hope you don't," Ruby said. "She's not like normal folks. There's something different about her. I didn't see it until it was too late. If I had, I might have turned her down when she asked me to join them. But I took the blood oath and I'm stuck."

"Blood oath?"

"She made each of us swear by the Bible. And then she cut our fingers and mixed the blood to seal the pact, as she put it."

"That's a new one," Fargo said.

"I told you. She'd not like any female you ever met. Or any male, for that matter."

"The others you mentioned," Fargo said. "Are they as new at being outlaws as you are?"

Ruby didn't answer right away. When she did, she said, "You know, I never thought of us like that, but I reckon we are. Outlaws. My ma would roll over in her grave if she knew how far I've sunk."

At that moment Geraldine Waxler brought her sorrel alongside the Ovaro. "What are you two talking about?"

"Nothing much," Fargo said.

"Why do I have the feeling you're holding something back on me?" Geraldine asked.

Fargo ignored the question and poked Ruby. "How far ahead are your friends?"

"Three or four hours. Maybe more."

"That's all?" Were it not for the heat, Fargo would push the Ovaro to overtake them.

"They have to be careful not to wear out the packhorses," Ruby said. "And to ration our water so it lasts."

That reminded Fargo. He'd been through this region before. He knew of a tank that few whites did. It never went dry.

"Everything was well thought out down to the smallest detail," Ruby said. "Not by me, you understand. I don't have the head for it. All that arithmetic and reading maps and such. She does, though."

"She?" Geraldine said.

Ruby frowned. "Damn me and my mouth."

Fargo expected Geraldine to quiz her but instead Geraldine pointed and said, "What's he up to?"

It was the Apache who had helped himself to Ruby's bay. He was just out of rifle range, pacing them.

"He's shadowing us," Fargo said.

"Out in the open like that?"

"He wants us to know he's there."

"Why?"

"You'd have to ask him," Fargo said. Sometimes Apaches liked to toy with their victim, like cats toyed with mice. But to show himself like that was unusual.

"As if we don't have enough to deal with," Geraldine said. "I thought he was long gone."

"Maybe it's me he's after," Ruby said.

Fargo hadn't thought of that. Maybe it wasn't mere chance that the warrior stole her horse. Maybe the Apache had been following her a while, biding his time.

"That gives me an idea," Geraldine said. "We should leave her for him to do whatever he wants and ride on while he's busy with her."

"You wouldn't," Ruby said.

"Sure I would," Geraldine said, and placed her hand on her revolver.

14

Fargo had been watching the Apache, but now he turned and said simply, "No."

"Why not?" Geraldine demanded. "It would be fitting after what she and those others did to Hank and his men."

"We might need her," was just one of the reasons Fargo had.

"For what? She won't cooperate. She won't tell us who else took part. We might as well be shed of her here and now."

"No, I said."

Geraldine didn't hide her resentment. "I am growing sick and tired of you telling me what I can and can't do."

"It was your idea to tag along," Fargo said, "and you agreed to do as I say."

"If I'd known you were so weak-kneed, I wouldn't have."

Fargo was tired of her carping. "You're letting your hate get the better of you. It will eat at you if you don't stop."

"I lost the man I loved more than any other," Geraldine said. "You're damn right I hate those who did it." Scowling, she slowed the sorrel and fell in behind him.

"You'd better keep an eye on her," Ruby said. "I don't trust her a lick."

Fargo doubted Geraldine would try anything just yet. Not until they caught up to the rest of the outlaws. "You're my prisoner. I won't let anything happen to you."

"If you figure that will endear me to you, you're mistaken. You have me belly down over your horse."

"I could gag you, too," Fargo said. Then he wouldn't have to listen to one of them, at least.

Ruby hung her head and closed her eyes.

To the north, the Apache continued to shadow them. He sat the horse with his head high and his chest out, almost as if he was taunting them to try to do something.

Fargo had never seen the like. But then again, he wouldn't put anything past Apaches. They lived by their own code, the rest of the world be damned.

Out of the blue Ruby remarked, "She really did love that major, didn't she?"

"More than anything," Fargo said.

"I've never been in love, myself. Oh, I've cared for a few gents here and there. But love? It's like something from one of those fairy tales. You know, where the prince sweeps some scullery maid off her feet and makes her a princess. How dumb is that?"

"Why are you telling me this?"

"I don't know. I'm bored hanging here. There's nothing else to do *but* talk," Ruby said.

"Then tell me about the other ladies in your gang."

"I'd better not. I told you about Big Bertha, didn't I?"

"Not her name, no."

"Damn it," Ruby said. "I did it again."

"Big Bertha?" Fargo repeated. The name was vaguely familiar. "I've heard that name before, somewhere."

"You won't get any more out of me. She'd beat me with a club."

"Robbing the payroll was her idea, I take it?" Fargo suspected. "She's the brains of the outfit."

"No, no, no," Ruby said.

"Wait a minute," Fargo said. In his mind's eye, he flashed back to a visit he paid to Saint Louis some time back. He rarely ventured that far east, and he'd treated himself to a night at a sporting house. "I met a dove by that handle once." Big Bertha was the madam of the place, a giant of a woman who cropped her hair short and smoked cigars. If he recollected rightly, she'd been in her forties. "But no. It couldn't be her. She'd be fifty by now."

"What does her age matter?" Ruby said. "Bertha is the toughest woman I ever met. She has more vinegar and vim than people half her age." She paused. "Whatever you do, don't tell Geraldine."

"Why not?"

"Just don't. And now that the cat is out of the bag, take my advice. Turn around and forget about recovering the money. You're a dead man if you don't."

"What do you care what happens to me?"

"Don't flatter yourself."

More time passed.

The Apache continued to play his little game. Once, when

Fargo veered toward him, the warrior moved the same distance away. When Fargo resumed riding to the northwest, the Apache moved back to where he had been before.

Geraldine was strangely quiet. A couple of times Fargo glanced back at her, and she gave him cold looks.

Fargo figured to stop along about sundown to put coffee on. Apache or no, their horses needed rest. He also hoped to spot Big Bertha's campfire.

The sun was a red inferno on the rim of the world when he drew rein atop a rise. "This will do to stop for the night."

Geraldine brought her sorrel up. "Fine by me."

"Over your sulk?" Fargo asked.

She didn't answer.

Dismounting, Fargo lifted Ruby off and set her on the ground. "Do I need to remind you to behave yourself?"

"Don't worry. I don't want a bullet in my back." Ruby was looking at Geraldine when she said it.

The Apache drew rein, too, off amid the mesquite, and watched as Fargo went about gathering brush for their fire.

"Why is he just sitting there?" Ruby said. "What is he up to?"

"Beats the hell out of me," Fargo admitted.

"Could be he's waiting for dark so he can slip in and do us in."

"Could be." Fargo plucked a handful of dry grass to use for kindling.

"It doesn't seem to bother you none."

"First things first," Fargo said.

"Whatever that means." Ruby sat up and adjusted her floppy hat. "Cut me loose and give me a gun and I'll help you when he jumps us."

Fargo chuckled.

"You don't believe me?"

Before Fargo could reply, Geraldine came over and stood watching him make the fire. "I've been thinking about it and thinking about it and I've come to a decision."

"About?" Fargo said without looking up. He puffed on a tiny flame and it grew larger.

"I shouldn't have promised you I'd do as you want. It never occurred to me that you'd go so easy on them."

"He hasn't been easy on me, dearie," Ruby said.

"Sure he has," Geraldine said. "You're still breathing, aren't you? No broken bones. No bruises. If that's not going easy, I don't know what is."

"You'd have beaten me black-and-blue by now, I suppose?"

"And a lot worse if you didn't tell me what I want to know."

"I'm glad you gave your word to him, then," Ruby said.

"About that," Geraldine said. "It's not as if my promise is etched in stone or anything."

Fargo, adding twigs to the kindling, heard Ruby gasp. Turning, he raised his head, and found himself staring into the muzzle of Geraldine's revolver. She smiled and cocked it.

"What's this?"

"I've decided this has gone on long enough. I'm taking over."

"Oh, hell," Ruby said.

Fargo was tempted to lunge, swat the six-shooter aside, and try to disarm her, but the revolver was liable to go off. "This is what I get for trusting you."

"It's your own fault. If you had listened to me, I wouldn't be doing this," Geraldine said.

"What about that Apache, you stupid cow?" Ruby snapped. "Without Fargo, how will you handle him?"

"I've given that some thought, too." Geraldine took a quick step back. "Your Colt, if you please, and even if you don't. Use two fingers and ease it from your holster nice and slow. This close, I can't hardly miss."

Fargo hesitated.

"If you're thinking I won't shoot, you're mistaken," Geraldine said. "I don't want to kill you if I can help it but I have no qualms about shooting you in the arm or the leg."

Fargo believed her.

"The thing is, if I hit a vein you might bleed out. Or the gun will kick and I'll shoot you in the chest by accident."

Fargo could easily see that happening.

"So if I were you I'd shed your hardware and be grateful I don't shoot you anyway."

"Go easy on that trigger," Fargo cautioned. Using his thumb and forefinger, he plucked his Colt out and set it down between them. "Happy now?"

"It's a start." Geraldine carefully slid her foot forward and kicked the Colt farther away. Then, backing to the Ovaro, she removed his rope, brought it over, and dropped it.

Fargo experienced a ripple of unease. "You're making a mistake."

"I've made them before." Geraldine shifted toward Ruby. "Your turn. Tie his hands and feet."

Ruby held up her arms. "With my wrists bound?"

"You can tie good enough. Get to it."

Sliding over, Ruby picked up the rope. "I'm sorry," she said.

"No jabbering. Just tie," Geraldine commanded. She took another step back and pointed her revolver at Fargo's chest. "I want to head out as soon as it's dark enough."

Ruby froze in the act of uncoiling the rope. "Head where?"

"After your friends. We'll take his horse and mine and leave him by the fire."

"He'll be helpless," Ruby said. "With that Apache out there."

"I'm counting on that to buy us time to get away," Geraldine informed her. "You'll lead me to your friends and I'll have the satisfaction of seeing them die gurgling their own blood."

Fargo had badly misjudged her. Her thirst for revenge had become an obsession. "Think about this, Geraldine. You need me."

"Not anymore. I have this cow. The only purpose you serve now is to keep that Apache distracted a while." Geraldine added regretfully, "I'm sorry. I truly am. You've left me no choice."

"You do this, you're no different than them," Fargo tried one last time.

"I know," Geraldine said. "But I can live with that." She motioned at Ruby. "Get to tying."

Ruby held the rope out toward Fargo. "Isn't life a bitch?" she said.

15

Skye Fargo simmered with fury. Being left to be butchered by an Apache was bad enough. Geraldine Waxler had also taken the Ovaro. At gunpoint she had forced Ruby to climb on the stallion, and together they'd ridden off into the night.

That was five minutes ago.

Fargo's hands were tied behind his back, his ankles bound, as well. Geraldine had made Ruby use a short length of rope to tie

64

his wrists and his ankles together so that when he pulled on his arms, it hurt his legs, and vice versa.

He couldn't reach the knots in the rope to pry them loose. He couldn't reach the toothpick in his boot, either.

Geraldine had done a good job of it. But she'd made one mistake. She'd left the fire burning. "So the Apache will see you're helpless," was how she put it.

The fire could also be Fargo's salvation.

He'd been waiting for their hoof falls to fade before he acted. He didn't want Geraldine to look back and catch him. She'd probably return to put the fire out.

The night was now quiet, save for the crackling of the flames.

Rolling over so his back was to the fire, Fargo wriggled closer. He accidentally moved too close and felt flame sear his hands. Jerking them away, he gritted his teeth to keep from crying out.

When the pain subsided, Fargo twisted his head and slowly slid his wrists close enough for the fire to lick at the rope. The heat was intense. New pain shot up his arms but it couldn't be helped. He was bound to be burned but he must free himself quickly. That Apache wouldn't wait long to move in.

The smell of burning flesh reached his nose. He tried to keep at it but the pain became unendurable. Pulling his hands back, he waited for the agony to fade.

Fargo glanced to the north. He swore he could feel the warrior's eyes on him. It spurred him into sliding his hands to the fire, pain or no pain. He saw smoke rise from the rope. Some of the strands were charred but not nearly enough. It was a new rope and new rope took longer to burn.

His fury at Geraldine was matched by his anger at his own lapse in judgment. He never should have let her come along. A moment of weakness, and now look.

The pain became excruciating. His skin was blackened in spots, and blisters were forming.

Hissing through his nose, Fargo refused to give up. It was literally a matter of life and death. The Apache wouldn't show him any mercy; he was just another white invader to be disposed of.

He listened for the sound of the warrior's horse but heard nothing. Maybe he'd be lucky. Maybe the warrior had gone off and not seen what Geraldine did. Or maybe the man had gone off after the women.

Once again he had to pull his hands away. Part of the rope was burnt but so were his wrists. They would hurt him for weeks.

Girding himself, Fargo was set to try again, when, from out of the corner of his eye, he caught movement. He looked up, his gut balling into a knot.

The Apache stood not six feet away. He'd come on foot, not on horseback. His rifle was in the crook of his arm, and he was regarding Fargo in amusement.

"Hell," Fargo said, and braced for the worst. He was completely helpless.

The Apache came nearer, his hand dropping to a knife on his left hip.

"Make it quick, damn you." Fargo had always known that one day something like this might happen but he'd always imagined he would go down fighting.

The warrior drew his knife.

Fargo would try to kick his legs out from under him, and once he had the Apache on the ground, sink his teeth into the man's neck. It was all he could do.

The Apache moved the blade back and forth. *"Tagoon-yah-dah."*

Fargo had lived with an Apache band once, and learned enough to translate. The warrior had just said, "You are a fool." Bristling, he replied, "Go to hell."

The Apache grinned.

"You speak the white tongue?" Fargo realized.

Squatting just out of reach, the warrior placed his rifle on the ground and rested his forearms on his knees. "I speak it good, white-eye."

Only then did Fargo notice that the warrior's eyes were blue; Apaches nearly always had brown or black eyes. The man's face wasn't typical of an Apache, either. The cheekbones were more prominent, the chin not rounded. "You're part white."

"My father Chiricahua. My mother was your kind."

Fargo had met more than a few half-breeds in his travels. As a rule they were looked down on, especially in the white world. "Do your folks live with the Chiricahuas?"

"Father and mother dead," the warrior said. "Killed in Mexico by scalp hunters."

Fargo had never taken part in the vile business of lifting scalps for bounty money but he was acquainted with a few who did. "A rotten way to die."

The warrior grunted.

"But then, there's no shortage of bastards in this world," Fargo declared. No shortage of bitches, either.

"Scalp hunters dead, too," the Apache said. "I hunt them. I find them." He moved the tip of the knife across his own throat without touching it.

"They got what they deserved," Fargo said.

"We think alike, white-eye."

Fargo was unsure what to make of how friendly the warrior was being. Most Apaches would have killed him by now, or started to carve on him to test his courage. "How are you called?"

"My white name John Jackson." The warrior paused. "Apaches call me Slits Throats."

So that's how he was going to do it, Fargo realized.

Slits Throats gestured. "Why did white women do this to you?"

"It's a long story," Fargo said.

"You going somewhere?"

Fargo would swear that inwardly the warrior was laughing at him. "You really want to hear it?"

"I never see white women tie a white man before. Why you not fight? You afraid of them?"

"The one pulled a gun on me. You must have seen her."

"Let me hear story."

Reluctantly, Fargo explained about the payroll robbery, about Mrs. Waxler, and about the five female outlaws.

"Five white women rob army?" Slits Throats said, and chuckled.

"How did you get mixed in this?" Fargo wanted to know.

"I came on tracks of woman on bay. I want her horse, so I stalk her. I see her try to shoot you, see you take her captive, see the other one tie you. This was strange, even for white-eyes. It make me curious."

"Now you know," Fargo said. "You might as well get it over with."

"Eh?"

"I don't like cat and mouse," Fargo said, "especially when I'm the mouse."

"You want me slit your throat?"

"That's what you aim to do, isn't it?"

"You first white-eye ever ask me to kill him," Slits Throats said, and his shoulders shook in silent mirth.

"Glad you're amused," Fargo said.

"You did hear me say my father white?"

"To some that wouldn't make a difference."

Slits Throats grew somber. "I not hate my father, white-eye. He loved my mother. He good father to me."

"What about other whites? What about me?"

"You make me laugh," Slits Throats said.

Fargo propped his elbows under him. "If you're not fixing to kill me, why haven't you cut me free?"

Slits Throats regarded him a bit. "I have—" He stopped. "What do whites call it? A *proposition* for you."

"I'm listening," Fargo said, smothering his bewilderment.

"I free you," Slits Throats said. "I help you track the white women. For that, you give me two things."

"If I can," Fargo said, wondering what in the world they could be.

"I want a horse."

"You have the bay."

"I want another horse."

Fargo was dumbfounded. Slits Throats could easily steal another from someone else. "That's easy enough. What else?"

"One hundred dollars."

Just when Fargo thought he'd heard everything. Apaches had little interest in money. But then, Slits Throats was part white. "The army can afford to pay that much as a reward, I reckon."

"Not army. You."

"You want me to pay you the hundred out of my own pocket?"

Slits Throats wagged his knife, and grinned. "Your life not worth that much?"

Fargo was thoroughly confused. The request made no sense. But who was he to quibble, the predicament he was in. "A horse and a hundred dollars. Agreed."

"We shake on it." Slits Throats moved around behind him.

The knife flashed, and the rope between Fargo's arms and legs was severed. Another flash, and the rope around his wrists fell off, his skin unbroken.

Sitting up, Fargo removed the rest of the rope himself. His blisters hurt like hell but he put them from his mind. "I'm obliged."

Slits Throats came back around, slid his knife into its sheath, and held out his callused hand. "We have a deal, as whites say?"

Fargo shook. "What will your Apache friends think, you helping a white man?"

"They do what they want. I do what I want. You savvy?"

Fargo had never cared what others thought, either. Some folks did. They lived their whole lives trying to fit in with everyone else. They'd wear the same clothes everybody else did, go about their day like everybody else. To be considered different was a calamity.

"When you want to start?" Slits Throats asked. "Now or first light?"

Rubbing his wrists, Fargo stood. Not a single light showed anywhere. If Big Bertha and her cohorts had stopped for the night, they were smart enough to hide their fire. "It will have to be daybreak."

"I be back," Slits Throats said, and melted into the darkness as soundlessly as a specter.

Fargo looked down at his empty holster. He wished he had his Colt but Geraldine had taken it. His Henry, too. All he had left was the toothpick.

It wasn't a minute later that hooves thudded, and Slits Throats returned on the bay. Hopping down, he patted it. "If you hungry, we can eat horse."

"No, thanks," Fargo said. Apaches often ate their animals, but he wasn't *that* hungry. "I would like to look in those saddlebags."

"Be my guest."

Fargo had to remember the warrior was half-white. He took the saddlebags and spread them by the fire and began taking everything out. "Coffee, by God." And a pot to make it in. He also found ammunition for Ruby's rifle, a spare man's shirt and britches, and the carmine she used on her lips as well as the brush she applied it with.

"What is that?" Slits Throats asked.

Fargo told him.

"Make mouth red? I want them."

Wondering what in the world the breed wanted them for, Fargo handed them over. "You should look right pretty."

"Not for me, silly white-eye," Slits Throats said. "For wife."

"You have one."

"Soon, maybe."

Fargo had more important things to ponder. Such as what he'd do when he caught up to Geraldine, to say nothing of the female outlaws. The way things had been going, the only thing he could say with certainty was that corralling them wouldn't be easy.

Matter of fact, the way things had been going, he'd be lucky to make it back to Fort Bowie alive.

16

Fargo slept fitfully. Half a pot of coffee was partly to blame. His new "partner" had more to do with it. He should be grateful that Slits Throats had freed him. He should be able to let down his guard long enough to get a few hours sleep. But try as he might, he couldn't. He'd doze off for a few minutes and snap awake again to see Slits Throats lying on the ground on the other side of the charred remains of their fire. He couldn't make out much detail in the dark but Fargo had the sense that the breed was awake and staring at him.

The first trace of dawn was cause for Fargo to get up and get the fire going. He needed the other half of that pot of coffee.

Slits Throats opened his eyes and sat up. "You not sleep much."

"My wrists," Fargo said by way of excuse. The blisters bothered him, but not that much.

"That only reason?"

"What else?" Fargo said. He had a sense that the breed was laughing at him again.

"Whites let pain hurt too much," Slits Throats said.

"No argument there," Fargo replied. He'd witnessed firsthand how Apaches could endure pain that would make most anyone else scream in torment.

"You like being white-eye?"

Fargo set the coffeepot so it would heat up, and shrugged. "I've never thought about it much."

"You think of it when you like me. Part white. Part red. Many hate those who half of each."

Since Slits Throats was being so gabby, Fargo decided to say, "I'm curious. What do you want the hundred dollars for?"

"Buy new rifle," Slits Throats said. He patted the Spencer in his lap. "This is good gun. It shoots true. But I want rifle like you have." His lips quirked. "Rifle woman take."

"Don't remind me."

"How it feel to be beat by woman?"

"I knew it," Fargo said. "You're rubbing it in. You're enjoying yourself, aren't you?"

"You funny man."

"I thought I was silly."

"You silly *and* funny," Slits Throats said. "Most white-eyes one or other. You both."

Fargo bit off a "Go to hell."

"Tell me about shiny rifle," Slits Throats said. "It called Henry, yes?"

"It's named after the man who came up with it, yes."

"It true that Henry shoot more times than Spencer?"

"A Henry holds sixteen rounds. A Spencer can only hold seven," Fargo confirmed.

Slits Throats' face lit with delight. "Sixteen," he repeated, almost in awe. "Can kill many times with gun like that."

"A Henry costs about forty dollars," Fargo mentioned. A little more if the buyer wanted a sling or extras, like having the receiver gold-plated instead of brass.

"And bullets?"

"Ten dollars will buy you a thousand rounds."

"Hundred dollars more than enough, then," Slits Throats said, clearly pleased. "Can buy Henry and much bullets."

"You really have your heart set on it," Fargo said.

"Many Chiricahuas have Spencer. Few have Henry."

Fargo thought he understood. To an Apache, owning a rifle like a Henry was a mark of prestige. Other warriors would secretly admire it, and want one of their own.

The coffee was soon ready, and Fargo savored his first cup. He offered some to Slits Throats but he wanted only a few swallows of water from Ruby's canteen.

A ring of orange crowned the eastern horizon when they were ready to head out. Fargo figured they'd ride double but Slits Throats surprised him.

"You ride. I run."

"You sure?"

"Me Apache."

"Suit yourself," Fargo said. Apache endurance was legendary. It was said an Apache could travel seventy-five miles in a day at a dogtrot.

The trail was easy to follow. They made good time.

It was soon apparent that Geraldine hadn't stopped for the

night. She should have. The Ovaro and the sorrel needed rest. By the middle of the day they would be flagging.

Not Slits Throats. He ran tirelessly, matching the fast walk of the bay, his breathing as normal as if he were taking a stroll.

The terrain became more mountainous.

Soon the hoofprints climbed toward an island of ponderosa pines, some of the trees over a hundred feet high.

Fargo wasn't quite to the trees when Slits Throats suddenly stopped.

"Voices."

Fargo drew rein. He strained his ears but he couldn't hear anything other than a few birds.

"Women," Slits Throats said. "They angry."

Fargo took his word for it. Dismounting, he led the bay, careful to avoid rocks that might clatter and give them away. The first small pine he came to, he tied the reins and crept into the shadowed woods. His hand drifted to his empty holster, and he frowned.

At his side glided Slits Throats.

They had gone over a hundred feet in when Fargo halted and crouched. He'd heard the voices too.

". . . tired of your griping," Ruby was saying. "You're still alive, aren't you?"

"You tricked me, you cow," Geraldine said bitterly.

"What the hell did you expect?"

Fargo stalked closer.

The women had stopped at a small clearing. There was shade from the sun, and something with even more appeal: a spring. The Ovaro and the sorrel were picketed close by, and a small fire gave off hardly any smoke. Ruby was hunkered beside it, drinking coffee she had brewed in Fargo's own pot, sipping from Fargo's own cup. Her rifle was at her feet, and she was grinning like the cat that just ate the canary.

Geraldine Waxler lay on the other side of the fire. Her wrists were tied. She had a gash in her temple, and a ribbon of dried blood ran from the gash to her chin. "I should never have turned my back on you."

"Did you think I was too scared to try and turn the tables? Did you think I was afraid of *you*?"

"You acted like you were."

"Jackass," Ruby said. "You're a whore, like me. What's to be afraid of?"

"So what now? You finish me off?"

"No," Ruby said. "I'm taking you to my boss. She'd like that, I do believe."

"She?"

"The person who organized the payroll robbery, the very one who shot your precious husband full of holes, is a woman."

"The hell you say."

Slits Throats nudged Fargo and whispered, "What we do?"

"We don't do anything yet," Fargo whispered. He hoped to overhear more.

In the clearing, Ruby was saying, "And before you ask, no, I won't tell you who the woman is. I want it to be a surprise."

Geraldine seemed dazed. "My husband could hold his own against Apaches. And he was shot by a female?"

"Women can be as deadly as men when they put their minds to it," Ruby boasted.

Fargo agreed. He'd run across some ladies who were as deadly as they came.

"What is this world coming to?" Geraldine said.

"Maybe you should ask that scout," Ruby said. "He was on your side, wasn't he? Helping you catch the ones who shot your major. And what did you do? Refresh my memory?"

Geraldine didn't respond.

"Now I remember," Ruby said, smirking. "You left him to be whittled on by an Apache. So don't lie there and claim the notion of a woman shooting your husband shocks you. You're not much different than she is."

"I couldn't let Fargo stop me."

"Is that your excuse?" Ruby taunted. "By now he's probably been skinned alive and strangled with his own innards." She shook her head in disgust. "If that's what you do to your friends, I'd hate to see what you do to your enemies."

"I wasn't thinking straight," Geraldine said.

"Liar," Ruby shot back. "You knew exactly what you were up to. And truth to tell, I should thank you. With him out of the way, you've made it a lot easier for me. He'd never have let me get the better of him."

"Lord, I am tired of your chatter."

"You can't stand to hear the truth, is more like it." Ruby raised Fargo's tin cup and took several swallows. "Ah. That hit the spot. I'd give you some but you're not getting a drop to drink until we've caught up to my friends."

"That could take days."

73

"At least," Ruby said.

"I'll die of thirst."

"One can only hope."

"But you just said you wanted to turn me over to your boss," Geraldine reminded her.

"I never said you had to be breathing."

"You'd kill me for no reason? How coldhearted are you?"

"No reason?" Ruby scoffed. "How about to keep you from killing us?"

Geraldine hung her head. "This isn't working out as I'd hoped."

Fargo had listened to enough. He wasn't learning anything new. He turned to whisper to Slits Throats that they should move in.

The warrior wasn't there.

"What the hell?" Fargo blurted. He looked back at the clearing just as a muscular figure in a headband and knee-high moccasins reared up behind Ruby.

Slits Throats.

Ruby never heard him. She was smirking at Geraldine when the stock of Slits Throats' Spencer connected with her skull.

Ruby's beautiful green eyes rolled up into her head, and she collapsed.

Geraldine had been forlornly staring into the fire but now she cried, "God in heaven! Not you! Not here!" She scrambled back in terror.

Slits Throats stepped over Ruby and came around the fire.

"Stay back!" Geraldine screeched, all her courage flown.

Fargo walked out of the ponderosas and planted himself behind her. She was as oblivious to him as she had been to Slits Throats.

Geraldine gave a start when she collided with his legs. Half turning, she bleated in surprise, "You!"

"Miss me?" Fargo said.

"How are you still alive? Why didn't that stupid Indian kill you?"

"You'll have to ask him when you wake up."

"Wake up?" Geraldine said in confusion.

Bending, Fargo slugged her on the jaw. He didn't use all his strength but one punch was all it took. She was out like a snuffed wick.

Slits Throats came up. "You look happy, white-eye."

"Happy as hell," Fargo said.

17

All was temporarily right with Fargo's world. He had the Ovaro back. He had the Henry. His Colt was in his holster.

He was seated at the fire Ruby had made, finishing the coffee she'd brewed. Both women were tied and lay to either side.

Slits Throats came over. "Women not come around yet?"

"My ears are grateful," Fargo said.

The warrior gazed skyward. "Much daylight left. I ride ahead. Find where others be."

"Don't let them see you."

Slits Throats snorted and turned toward the horses.

"Watch out for Apaches," Fargo said.

Slits Throats looked back and laughed. "See? You one funny white-eye."

"I try," Fargo told him.

The warrior left and ten minutes went by, ten minutes of blessed peace and quiet. Then Geraldine Waxler groaned and slowly raised her head, looking around in confusion. She saw Fargo, and her face hardened in anger. "You hit me."

"I sure as hell did."

"Don't sound so proud of it," Geraldine snapped.

"You tried to have me killed," Fargo said. "What did you think I'd do if I saw you again? Give you a big hug and a kiss?"

"I'm sorry about that."

"Sure you are." Fargo had made the mistake of trusting her once. He wouldn't make that mistake again.

"I can understand you being upset. . . ."

"Upset?" Fargo said. "I'd be dead now except that the Apache you counted on to do me in is part white himself and wanted me alive."

"How about that?" Geraldine said.

"Don't sound so disappointed."

"If you want my opinion . . ."

"I don't."

"I think you're overreacting."

"How's your jaw?"

That shut her up.

Fargo had other matters to think about. The first was that having two prisoners would slow him. The other was that the Ovaro and the sorrel could use another hour or so of rest, which would delay him even more. Since it couldn't be helped, he mentally shrugged and went on relaxing with his coffee.

Presently it was Ruby's turn to stir. She groaned louder than Geraldine had, and lifted her head more slowly. Her confusion was worse, too. She stared at Fargo for fully half a minute before recognition dawned and she came to her senses. "You bastard! You hit me from behind."

"I cannot tell a lie," Fargo said. "It wasn't me."

"Who else?" Ruby turned to Geraldine and scowled. "It couldn't have been her. She was tied up."

"It was my new pard," Fargo said. "The one who was following you. Who stole your horse."

"You don't mean that redskin?"

"The very same. His name is Slits Throats. When he comes back, you might want to thank him for not slitting yours."

"Thank him? Hell, he about busted my skull." Grimacing, Ruby struggled to a sitting position. She touched her bound hands to her head and winced. "I've got a hen's egg."

"Maybe it knocked some sense into you," Fargo said.

"He thinks he's funny," Geraldine said.

"Why does everyone keep saying that?" Fargo asked.

"I don't think you're funny," Ruby snarled.

"Thank you," Fargo said.

Geraldine laughed, then said, "Damn."

"You're both loco," Ruby said. "If my hands were free I'd blow out your wicks and leap for joy when it was done."

"Why are you mad at me?" Geraldine said. "I wasn't the one who bashed you over the noggin."

"Have you forgotten you were hauling me around at gunpoint?"

"I didn't hurt you, did I? Seems to me you should be grateful," Geraldine said.

Ruby looked as if she was about to explode. "Do you ever listen to yourself, you cow?"

"Ladies," Fargo said.

"Who are you calling a 'cow,' you pig?" Geraldine said. "What do you know about anything, anyhow?"

"Ladies?" Fargo said, louder.

"I know your type, bitch," Ruby said. "You were one of those doves who gussied herself up all the time and pranced around like she was the Almighty's gift to Creation."

"Ladies, damn it," Fargo said.

"And I know your type," Geraldine declared. "You're one of those who doesn't much care how she looks. You do just enough to get by because you're too lazy to better yourself."

Fargo let out a roar worthy of a grizzly. *"Ladies!"*

They both looked at him and Geraldine said, "What's the matter with you?"

"Not one more word out of either of you unless I say you can talk."

"What will you do?" Geraldine taunted. "Pistol-whip us?"

Fargo held up his fist.

"Oh," she said.

That bought half an hour of wonderful quiet. Fargo roused when the Ovaro whinnied, and Slits Throats rode out of the trees and vaulted down with the agile grace of a panther.

"You're back sooner than I thought you'd be," Fargo said.

Slits Throats was about to reply when he saw that the women had recovered. Coming around the fire, he studied the pair intently.

"What the hell are you looking at, you red devil?" Ruby demanded.

"White women," Slits Throats said.

"What did you find out?" Fargo asked.

Geraldine thrust her jaw at Slits Throats. "Yes, we're white, and we won't abide any of your heathen ways. You keep your hands to yourself—you hear me?"

"You have spirit," Slits Throats said. "I like that."

"Slits Throats?" Fargo said.

Ruby rose onto her knees. "What do I have? I must have something because you were following me."

"Big tits," Slits Throats said.

Ruby looked down at herself. "How can you tell, as loose as this shirt is?"

"Damn it to hell," Fargo said, and looked at the Ovaro. "Am I whispering and don't know it?" Picking up the coffeepot, he banged his cup against it.

The three of them turned.

"Why you do that, white-eye?" Slits Throats asked.

"He's peculiar," Geraldine said. "I didn't realize it when I met him but the more I get to know him, the more I see how strange he is."

"All whites strange," Slits Throats said.

"He's grumpy, too," Ruby said. "He yelled at us a while ago for nothing at all."

"Ladies," Fargo said. "Shut the hell up."

"See what I mean?" Ruby said.

Fargo focused on Slits Throats. "What did you find out?"

"You want good news or bad news?" the warrior said.

"What I want is a bottle of whiskey," Fargo said. "But let me hear it."

"Tracks say women who stole money far ahead. We not catch till late tomorrow."

"What's the good news?"

"That was the good," Slits Throats said. "The bad is that four Apaches cut trail and follow them."

"Make that two bottles," Fargo said.

"Eh?"

"Nothing. How far ahead are the Apaches?"

"Two hours. Maybe three. They on foot but that not slow them much."

"No," Fargo agreed. "It won't."

This affair was turning into a debacle. He was teamed up with a partner he didn't need, saddled with two women he'd rather be without, and now had an Apache war party as well as the female outlaws to deal with. "When it rains, it pours."

"Not rain for many sleeps," Slits Throats said. "This summer."

"Did you just tell a joke?"

"What that?"

"I give up," Fargo said, and stood. So much for letting the Ovaro and the sorrel rest a while longer. With Apaches after the outlaws, they needed to head right out.

After dousing the fire, Fargo put his pot and cup in his saddle-bags and brought the horses over. Before Geraldine could guess what he was up to, he scooped her into his arms and threw her over the sorrel belly down, as he'd done with Ruby the day before. Geraldine swore and struggled as he tied a rope from her wrists to her ankles, under the sorrel's belly.

"Don't do this, consarn you. I'm not an outlaw like she is. I deserve better treatment."

"What you deserve," Fargo said, "is another pop on the jaw." He went to Ruby, squatted, and untied her ankles. She seemed surprised, even more so when he took her arm and assisted her to her feet. "You get to ride double with me."

"I do?"

Fargo cupped his hands. "I'll give you a boost."

Ruby regarded him suspiciously. "Why are you being so nice all of a sudden?"

"I can throw you over the sorrel with Geraldine if you want."

"No, no," Ruby said quickly. She placed her shoe in his palm, and he swung her up and over.

"Slide back," Fargo said. When she did, he forked leather, snagged the sorrel's reins, and resumed the pursuit.

Slits Throats offered to ride ahead and keep an eye out for the Apaches and jabbed his heels to the bay.

No sooner was the warrior out of sight than Ruby snuggled against Fargo's back. "This is kind of cozy, ain't it?"

The feel of her breasts and the warmth of her body stirred Fargo, down low.

"Don't you think it's cozy?" she asked again, touching a finger to the nape of his neck.

"What are you up to?" Fargo said.

"Sweet little me?" Ruby replied, her breath fluttering his skin. "I'm as innocent as can be."

Fargo grinned. Things had become a lot more interesting.

18

They stopped for the night in chaparral country. A bluff offered shelter from the wind. There was no water other than the water in their canteens.

Geraldine was in a foul temper. When Fargo slid her off the

sorrel, she tried to bash his face with her elbow. As he set her down, she kicked at his leg. He was tempted to slug her again but didn't. "Behave, damn it."

"Do you have any idea what it was like, slung over that saddle all day? I'm chafed and sore and half sick."

"You brought this on yourself," Fargo said. She'd get no sympathy from him whatsoever.

"What if I promise to do whatever you tell me from here on out? Will you untie and let me ride tomorrow?"

"No."

Geraldine's invective would make a river rat proud. She ended with, "Keep treating me like this and there will be hell to pay."

As Fargo set to kindling a fire, Ruby turned to Geraldine and said, "You are one haughty bitch."

"What do you know?" Geraldine shot back.

"I know you have only yourself to blame for everything that's happened to you," Ruby said, "including the death of your husband."

Geraldine's nostrils flared like a riled buffalo's. "If I had a gun, I'd shoot you. That's a despicable thing to say."

"That's enough," Fargo growled. He wasn't going to put up with them bickering all night.

"Fine by me, handsome," Ruby said. "I'm not the one with a broom up her ass."

"If it's the last thing I ever do, I'll kill you," Geraldine vowed.

Fargo remembered her shoving that derringer in his face when they first met. He should have known then and there that she was about as levelheaded as a rabid she-wolf. "When will I learn?" he said to himself.

He set about putting coffee on, then rummaged in his saddlebags for a bundle of jerked venison. He gave several pieces to each of them.

Ruby thanked him.

Geraldine glared, but took them anyway.

Twilight descended. Fargo chewed on jerky and listened to the crackle of the fire and the distant lament of a coyote.

Ruby finished eating and asked for more. "I've never had this before. It's kind of tasty."

"You've never had jerky?"

"I was raised a city gal. Jerky is for farmers and hunters and whoever."

Fargo supposed it was.

Ruby bit into a new piece, her eyes twinkling. "You treated me decent today. I'm grateful."

"You behaved," Fargo said, and gave Geraldine a pointed look.

"I hope there're no hard feelings over my trying to shoot you. To be honest, my heart wasn't really in it."

"You could have fooled me," Fargo said.

"This outlaw business," Ruby said. "I'm not really cut out for it. I like my comforts. A soft bed. A willing man. A night of lovemaking." She grinned and winked.

"Yet here you are."

"What can I say?" Ruby gazed wistfully into the fire. "I like money as much as the next person. My share of the payroll is six thousand dollars. That's more than I'd make in ten years of selling my body for pokes."

A hoof thudded, and Fargo was on his feet in a twinkling, the Colt in his hand. But it was only Slits Throats, leading the bay by the reins.

"Good news or bad news?" Fargo asked.

"Four Chiricahuas make camp. They in no hurry. White women not get away."

"What will those Apaches do?" Ruby anxiously asked. "Kill them outright?"

Slits Throats shrugged. "Not know. Maybe kill. Maybe take to wickiup."

"A couple of those gals are good friends. I'd hate for them to come to harm."

Slits Throats turned to Fargo. "How about I go . . . What is white word? Spy on them?"

"You're a busy bee," Fargo said.

"Eh?"

"Spy to your heart's content." Fargo had no objections. It would be nice to know what the warriors intended to do.

Without another word, Slits Throats climbed on the bay and rode off into the dark.

Fargo still didn't know what to make of how reasonable the breed was being. It was almost unnatural. He couldn't help wondering if there was more to it than Slits Throats let on.

"Penny for your thoughts," Ruby said.

"You should get some rest. Both of you. We're heading out at first light and we'll be in the saddle all day."

"I never have needed that much sleep," Ruby said. "It's why I'm so frisky under the sheets."

"Too bad we don't have a bed handy," Fargo joked.

"Who needs one?"

Fargo imagined her without that bulky shirt and those britches, and felt a familiar urge.

Ruby bent toward him. "Did you hear me?"

Geraldine said in contempt, "Throw yourself at him, why don't you?"

"Stay out of this."

Geraldine said to Fargo, "You can do better than a cheap tart like her."

"I'll have you know I can get top dollar anytime, cow," Ruby said.

"There's no accounting for taste."

Fargo did as he'd done the night before and whacked the coffeepot with his almost empty cup. "You two are doing it again. Keep it up and I'll gag you."

"So?" Geraldine said.

"With a dirty sock."

Geraldine sniffed as if she could smell it. "Yes, I believe you would. You're not the gentleman I took you for. You're not like my poor Hank at all."

"Never claimed to be."

"That's telling her," Ruby said, and laughed.

"It goes for you, too," Fargo said.

"Well, hell," Ruby said.

Fargo spent the next fifteen minutes hobbling the Ovaro and the sorrel and walking in a wide circle to look and listen. The night was deceptively still.

As he reclaimed his seat, he noticed Ruby studying him.

"Mind if I ask a question?"

"Not when you're polite about it."

"What *do* you plan to do when you catch up to my friends? I won't stand by and let you gun them down."

"I aim to take them back to Fort Bowie."

"And if they won't go?"

"That's up to them."

"In other words, you'll shoot them if you have to."

"I sure as hell won't let them shoot me."

"You could have killed me back when I ambushed you. But you didn't. How come?"

"You're complaining?"

Leaning back, Fargo let himself relax. Between the jerky and the warmth of the fire and the long day he'd had, he began to feel drowsy. Yawning, he shook himself.

"You're not going to fall asleep on me, are you?" Ruby teased.

"Ladies first."

Geraldine muttered something and rolled over so her back was to them. "A bitch in heat and a bull in rut."

Ruby colored and went to reply but Fargo wagged a finger and she clammed up.

Fargo did more yawning. He refused to sleep until both women had turned in.

Close by, an owl hooted.

Instantly alert, Fargo sat up. Sometimes an owl wasn't what it seemed. Apaches were masters at imitating bird calls. He listened, scarcely breathing, for more hoots.

"What's the matter?" Ruby whispered.

"We might have company."

"Lord, no." Ruby slid closer, pressing her side to his leg. "You can't keep me tied. I need to be able to defend myself."

"I don't know as it's them yet."

Ruby gripped his pants and glanced about them in fear.

A twinge of conscience compelled Fargo to move his hand down his leg to his boot. He was about to unsheathe the toothpick when he recollected how little fear Ruby had shown of Slits Throats, or anything else, for that matter. A suspicion came over him. "Apaches scare you, do they?"

"They scare anyone with half a brain," Ruby said.

"Yet you were by your lonesome when I ran into you," Fargo mentioned. Few men, let alone women, would wander alone in Apache territory.

"I was scared then, too."

Fargo doubted it. He had a hunch she wasn't above a little playacting.

"Stay close to me, would you?" Ruby said, placing her hands on his thigh.

Fargo humored her, and him, by putting his arm around her shoulders. "I won't let anything happen to you."

"Thank you." Scooting higher, Ruby pecked him on the cheek and nestled hers on his chest. "I feel safer already."

"I feel something, too."

"You do? What?"

Fargo reached down, took hold of her hands, and placed them between his legs.

19

"Oh my," Ruby said. "We should do something about that." She glanced at Geraldine. "As soon as you know who falls asleep."

"Why wait?" Reaching up, he cupped one of her breasts. She had nothing on under the shirt, and he could feel the soft fullness of her globe and her taut nipple against his palm.

"Oh, you naughty man, you."

Fargo lowered his lips to her neck. "You haven't seen naughty yet."

Squirming, Ruby grinned and stroked him, down low. "You want to do it right here where she can see?"

No, Fargo didn't. Geraldine would likely throw a fit, and he could do without the aggravation. Rising, he pulled Ruby up, stuck a finger to his lips to caution silence, and moved quietly along the bottom of the bluff until they were out of the ring of firelight. Stopping, he pressed her against the rock wall. "Will this do?"

"Makes no never mind to me," Ruby said. "You wouldn't believe some of the places I've done it." She wriggled her bound wrists. "But what about my hands?"

"What about them?"

"It'd be a lot more fun if they were free."

Fargo shook his head. "Nice try."

"What? You think I excited you to trick you into untying me? I wouldn't do a thing like that."

Fargo nuzzled her neck.

"You're really not going to untie me, are you?"

Fargo ran the tip of his tongue from one side of her throat to the other.

"I give my word I won't try anything."

Fargo nipped her earlobe and felt her shiver.

"Don't blame me if I can't touch all the places you might want me to."

84

"I won't." Fargo kneaded each breast through her shirt. Her nipples became tacks, and she ground her hips against his.

"Last chance. Free me and I'll be a regular wildcat. You won't regret it."

"No." Fargo peeled her buttons free while lightly kissing her chin and her cheek.

"Damn you."

"We can go back if you want," Fargo said. "I never force a lady if she's not in the mood." He tweaked a nipple between his thumb and forefinger.

"Oh, I want to, all right, sugar," Ruby said, and melted into him.

Fargo pulled at her shirt, tugging it free of her pants. Sliding his hand underneath, he caressed her smooth belly, then roamed higher. Her breasts were swollen with desire. Cupping one, he elicited a moan.

"Lordy, you get me hot," Ruby breathed in his ear. She raised her arms above their heads. "Do me, handsome. Do me like you've never done anyone."

Fargo hoped she wasn't a talker. One of his peeves was women who gabbed while making love. To shut her up he locked his mouth to hers. Her lips parted, and her tongue met his.

Fargo glanced toward the fire. Geraldine hadn't moved. The rising and falling of her shoulder as she breathed suggested she was sound asleep. He was about to devote his entire attention to Ruby when the gleam of brass caused him to curse his stupidity. He'd left the Henry propped against the bluff.

All Geraldine had to do was roll over, scoot around the fire, and grab it. She wouldn't be able to use it effectively with her wrists tied, but still. He considered going to get it, but just then Ruby ran her knee up and down his thighs.

"Did you change your mind? You're not doing much."

Fargo remedied that. He resumed kneading her breasts, turning slightly so he could see the Henry and Geraldine. He still had his Colt and could stop her if she tried for it.

"That's better," Ruby whispered.

The last button gave, and her shirt parted.

Fargo admired her mounds, then inhaled a nipple and sucked it as if it were a piece of hard molasses. Ruby, panting, dropped her arms around his head and neck.

"Oh, I like that. But don't forget I have two."

Fargo didn't. He lathered one breast and then the other, his hands busy with her belt buckle. He got it undone and began to push her pants down, wondering what she might have on underneath. The answer: nothing.

"Getting right to it, are you?" Ruby said in his ear. "That's all right. I like it quick. I like it slow. I like it any way at all."

Fargo got her pants down around her knees. That would have to do. She couldn't spread her legs and wrap them around him but she could part them wide enough for what came next.

"Touch me where I want it most," Ruby breathlessly requested. "I want to feel you there."

Fargo slid a finger between her legs. She was dripping wet and hot as a furnace.

"Ohhhh yessssss."

Parting her nether lips, Fargo rubbed.

"Yes. Yes." Gasping, Ruby arched her back. "Right there. That's it."

Fargo inserted a finger, and she thrust herself against him so hard, they both nearly lost their balance. At his first stroke she sank her teeth into his shoulder, and if not for his buckskins, she would have bitten deep enough to draw blood.

Raising her head, Ruby purred, "Do me. Do me hard."

With his other hand, Fargo loosened his belt and lowered his pants. His manhood throbbed with his need. Spreading her legs as far as they would go, he pressed himself between her legs and rubbed the tip of his pole across her slit.

A hungry look came into her eyes. "I want you in me. I want you in me now."

With a sharp thrust, Fargo buried himself in her yielding tunnel. Ruby threw back her head and for a few moments he thought she would cry out and wake Geraldine, but she only sucked in a long breath and shook from her hair to her toes.

"You feel so good."

Covering a breast with his hand, Fargo bent his mouth to the other. At the same time he tucked at the knees and rammed up into her.

Just like that, Ruby spurted. She gripped his shoulders and humped fiercely, seeming surprised at her sudden release. She kept saying, "Oh! Oh! Oh!" the whole time.

Fargo let her grind herself out, and at length she sagged against him, her head on his shoulders.

"Whew. That took a lot out of me. I must have wanted it even more than I thought."

Fargo went on stroking.

Ruby's eyes widened slightly and she kissed the side of his neck. "You're a damn stallion," she breathed.

Placing his hands on the rock face behind her for leverage, Fargo pumped faster.

"What you do to me," Ruby said.

Fargo wished she would shut up. He checked on Geraldine once more to be sure she was still asleep, and let himself go, ramming into Ruby again and again.

She closed her eyes and licked her lips and gyrated her hips with abandon.

Fargo was on the cusp of exploding but she beat him to it with her second orgasm. Mewing like a kitten, she convulsed to an inner quake. It triggered his own release.

Eventually they coasted to a stop. Ruby grinned, kissed him on the lips, and said, "Not bad."

Extricating himself, Fargo pulled himself together, adjusted his gun belt, and turned.

Geraldine was on an elbow, glaring in their direction. "What did I say? You're like a bull in rut."

"And proud of it," Fargo said.

Ruby froze in the act of buttoning her shirt. "You were awake the whole time?"

"What if I was?" Geraldine said.

Fargo was glad she hadn't gone for the Henry. She could have shot him. He wouldn't have realized she had the rifle until it was too late.

"You can't see us," Ruby said. "The light doesn't reach this far."

"I could hear you," Geraldine said "That was enough."

Fargo strode to the fire and reclaimed the Henry. Sitting cross-legged, he put the rifle in his lap and refilled his tin cup.

"I can't tell you how disappointed I am in you," Geraldine said.

"I can't tell you how much I don't give a damn."

"I took you for a gentleman, like my Hank. I guess I was mistaken."

"You can shut up now," Fargo said.

Ruby came out of the dark tucking her shirt into her pants. It was awkward for her to do with her wrists bound but she managed. "I hope we gave you an earful, bitch."

"Don't you start, either," Fargo said.

"The airs she puts on," Ruby said. "Until she married her precious Hank, she was just another dove, like me."

"I was never like you," Geraldine said. "I had more class."

Ruby snorted. "You wouldn't know class if someone shoved it up your . . ."

"When I said enough," Fargo curtly cut in, "I meant it."

Shrugging, Ruby sat an arm's length away and scraped at the dirt with a fingernail. "It's hard for me to hold it in. She makes me so mad, looking down her nose at me like she does."

Geraldine sneered at Fargo. "I can't wait to tell the colonel about your dalliance."

"As if he'd give a damn," Fargo said.

"I don't know every army rule and regulation but there has to be one against having sex with a prisoner."

"How petty of you," Ruby said, scraping the dirt harder.

"After all he's put me through, any trouble I can get him in, I will."

Ruby put her hands on the ground and leaned on them. To Fargo she said, "Are you as tired of hearing her flap her gums as I am?"

Fargo wearily sighed. "You have no idea."

"Well, you won't have to listen to her much longer, if all goes like I hope it will."

"Oh?" Fargo said.

"Yes," Ruby said, nodding. "As soon as I get free, I aim to kill her. Of course, first I have to kill you." And with that, she threw the dirt she had scraped into his face.

20

Two handfuls caught Fargo full in the eyes. He instinctively recoiled. His vision blurring, he raised his hands to wipe the dirt away. He heard Geraldine yell for him to "Watch out!" and saw Ruby hurtling at him with her shoulder down. His chest exploded with pain, and he was smashed against the bluff.

Half blinded, desperate, Fargo clutched at the Henry and felt someone try to tug it out of his hand.

Ruby had hold of the stock.

Blinking furiously, Fargo tried to stand. He wasn't prepared for the knee that caught him in the gut. Doubling over, he managed to hold on to the Henry. Another kick missed his knee but sent pain shooting up and down his leg.

"Let go, damn you!" Ruby snarled.

The venom in Ruby's voice surprised Fargo as much as the dirt in his face. Not five minutes ago they'd made love, and here she was, trying to kill him. Belatedly, it dawned on him that she had let him have his way with her so she could take him unawares. She'd wanted him to think she could be trusted. And like a fool, he'd fallen for it.

Fargo's vision cleared just as her foot swept at his crotch. He absorbed the blow on his hip but it still hurt. He made it to his feet, firmed his hold on the Henry, and pulled with all his might.

"No!" Ruby cried as she stumbled and almost lost her grip. "I won't let you."

Thrusting his boot out, Fargo yanked, trying to trip her. Ruby stumbled and fell to her knees. He wrenched on the Henry but all he succeeded in doing was lifting her partway off the ground.

Ruby's face was close to his leg. Gaping her mouth wide, she bit him.

Fargo had been bitten before but never a bite that hurt as bad. He tried to jerk free and fell against the bluff.

Ruby ground her teeth like a wolf gnawing a bone.

Driving his knee into her temple, Fargo knocked her back. Taking advantage, he pulled on the Henry and lurched toward the fire. He expected her to cling to the rifle, and she did.

Ruby struggled mightily. She wasn't about to give up, and didn't realize what he was up to.

Fargo swung her into the fire.

In a panic, Ruby screamed.

Fargo had counted on it scaring her. He'd also counted on her doing what she did next—letting go of the Henry, she scrambled out of the fire to keep from being burned.

Fargo gripped the Henry like a club. He wasn't feeling merciful. As she started to stand he struck her across the head and felled her in her tracks.

"Took you long enough," Geraldine said.

"I don't want to hear it," Fargo growled. Every sinew hurting, he stepped to his saddle, and his rope.

"For a bit there I thought she had you."

"What would you care?" Fargo retorted.

"About you? Not a lick. But if she'd gotten hold of your rifle, she'd have shot me after she shot you."

"You're welcome for saving your bacon."

"Hell. You barely saved your own."

Wrapping one end of the rope around Ruby's ankles, Fargo ran coil after coil up the entire length of her long legs to her waist. Several knots ensured it wouldn't come undone.

"Gag her while you're at it," Geraldine said. "I'm tired of listening to her voice."

"I'm tired of listening to yours."

"Why are you picking on me? I tried to warn you, didn't I?"

"To save your own hide."

Suddenly weary, Fargo reclaimed his seat by the bluff. His tin cup was in the dirt, and he had to wash it off before he could use it.

"At least now you know I'm not your real enemy," Geraldine said. "The outlaws are."

"The only friend I have is right there," Fargo said, and pointed at the Ovaro.

"I'm not out to do you harm," Geraldine insisted.

"Could have fooled me."

"I was afraid you'd try to stop me, and I made a mistake. How many times must I say it?"

"You're making another."

"Oh?"

"If you don't shut the hell up," Fargo said, "I'll do to you what I just did to her."

Geraldine scowled and turned away.

Refilling his cup, Fargo gratefully swallowed. He had blood on his cheek from where Ruby had scratched him, and blood on his leg from where she'd bit him. His ribs ached, his hip hurt, and his head throbbed when he moved it. He decided to sit there a while and not do a thing except berate himself for being the biggest jackass west of the Mississippi River.

Ruby revived sooner than he reckoned. Muttering, she tried to sit up, discovered she was practically wrapped in rope from her waist to her toes, and swore. Looking over at him, she growled, "You son of a bitch."

"I don't see what you have to gripe about," Fargo said. "You're still alive."

Wriggling furiously, Ruby swung herself around and flexed her legs as if she were contemplating trying to kick him.

"I'll break both of them," Fargo said.

Her mouth a slit, Ruby let her legs sink to the ground. "I almost had you. If I'd had a rock to bean you with instead of just dirt, your brains would be leaking out."

"You had me fooled," Fargo admitted.

"What did you expect? That I'd let you turn me over to the army? That I'd spend the rest of my life behind bars? Or, worse yet, end my days at the end of a rope?"

"I hope it's that," Fargo said.

"Of course you do. You're a man, and men have it easy. You have no notion of how hard it's been for me. How I've had to work twice as hard just to make ends meet."

"Do I break out a violin now or later?"

"For once in my life I stand to get ahead. To have more money than I ever had scrimping and saving. Enough to last a lifetime."

"You think it is." Fargo's personal experience had been that money was like water. It ran through his hands much too easily.

"Six thousand dollars," Ruby said. "I'll do anything to get it. Kill. Steal. Trick a stupid scout so I can bash in his skull."

"That's the Ruby I know and love."

"Go to hell."

Fargo wondered if the other outlaws were as fanatical about their share of the loot as she was. If so, it didn't bode well.

"You've licked me but you won't lick my friend. They'll do to you as they did those blue coats. Just see if they don't."

"Lights out," Fargo said.

"You're putting out the fire?"

"It's what they say at an army post when the soldiers in the barracks have to turn in," Fargo explained.

"You're saying you want me to shut up?"

"You don't have to if you don't want to." Fargo patted the Henry. "I'd be glad to do it for you."

Now Fargo had two sulking women on his hands. One motivated by revenge, the other by greed.

To him this was a job, nothing more. A job that became more and more complicated as time went on.

The solution was to take it one step at a time. The first step was to deal with the Apaches stalking the women. The second was to deal with the women. It would be nice to take them alive but if he couldn't, he couldn't. Afterward, he'd return the stolen payroll to the army, and get on with his life.

Easy as pie, Fargo thought, and grinned.

The stars were out in force and the wind had picked up. Sheltered by the bluff, their fire crackled undisturbed.

Fargo would like to turn in but he had his prisoners to consider. Binding them wasn't enough. He wouldn't put it past one or the other to wait until he was asleep and rip out his throat with their teeth.

There was still some rope left. Getting up, Fargo went to Ruby. She lay with her cheek on the ground and her eyes closed. Stooping, he grabbed her by her heels.

"What the hell?" Ruby squawked, trying to turn. "What do you think you're doing?"

Fargo dragged her over to Geraldine and positioned them so their feet were practically touching.

"What *are* you doing?" Geraldine asked. She had been watching him.

Hunkering, Fargo commenced to tie one end of the rope around Ruby's ankles.

"Let go of me," she hollered, and tried to pull away.

Holding firm, Fargo said, "We can do this with pain or without. Which will it be?"

Ruby had quite a vocabulary when it came to cuss words. But she didn't fight him as he tied a couple of tight knots. "What good did that do?"

"Don't you see?" Geraldine said as Fargo reached for her legs. "He's tying our feet together to make it next to impossible for us to sneak up on him in the middle of the night and do him in."

"He thinks he's so damn clever," Ruby said.

"He is," Geraldine said.

Fargo finished tying. Their legs were now bound fast together. One couldn't move without the other. And with their wrists tied, too, they couldn't get at him unless they undid the ropes—which would be next to impossible, as tight as the knots were. Smiling, he stood and moved back.

"Pleased with yourself, are you?" Ruby said. "Enjoy it while you can. Because as God is my witness, before this is over, you'll be as dead as dead can be."

21

The next day was more of the same, only Fargo had two women draped over saddles instead of one. They hated it. Ruby lit into him with that mouth of hers so he gagged both of them, too.

"Why are you gagging me?" Geraldine demanded as he was about to do her. "I haven't said a word."

"I'm looking forward to some peace and quiet."

"What if I give you my word I won't let out a peep?"

"I'd believe you," Fargo said, and gagged her.

The day wasn't quite as hot, which was a relief, and the trail left by Big Bertha's gang was as plain as ever.

He saw no track of the Apaches.

By noon he'd covered a lot of miles and reined up to rest the horses.

Dismounting, he placed both women on the ground, removed their gags, and offered water from his canteen.

Ruby glared with every swallow. When he pulled the canteen away to keep her from drinking too much, she smiled and said with mock sincerity, "Thank you."

Geraldine swallowed only once. "That's enough for me, thank you," she said. "We don't want to run out."

Fargo didn't have any. He sat where he could watch them and the horses, both. A bee buzzed past, so close he could have snatched it out of the air.

Swiping at a bang, Geraldine said, "I must be getting used to riding on my stomach. It didn't hurt as much today as it did yesterday."

Ruby was still glaring. "All this trouble you're going to, and what good will it do you?"

"Don't start," Fargo said.

"What does the money matter to you? Why risk your hide when it's not even yours?"

"You're forgetting the soldiers you killed."

"Men you didn't know, as I recollect," Ruby said. "At least this pathetic fool has a reason for being here."

"Why am I a fool?" Geraldine asked.

"You're putting your life in danger for a man you were only married to for, what was it, six months?"

"He loved me."

"Did you love him?"

Fargo was surprised when Geraldine hesitated.

"He was willing to forget my past. To overlook all I'd done. Do you realize how rare that was?"

"You didn't answer my question."

"Yes, I loved him."

"It sounds like you were grateful more than anything," Ruby said. "Is that worth dying for?"

"No more," Fargo said. He was so tired of their spats, he could scream.

Ruby glanced at the bandanna he'd used to gag her, and subsided, her face a mirror of raw hatred.

Fargo went to lean back when he heard a slight sound behind him. It sounded like the scratch of a moccasin sole, and he whirled, drawing his Colt as he spun. But it was only a rattler, winding about the brush. It paid no heed to them and soon slithered away.

Fargo was glad it hadn't spooked the horses. Shoving the Colt into his holster, he removed his hat and ran a hand through his sweat-soaked hair.

Fargo had to hand it to Big Bertha, whoever she was. She'd chosen her escape route well. Most would have stuck to what few roads there were, but not her. They were well off the beaten pathways between settlements, in a remote region few whites had ever set foot in.

To the northwest reared hills. Beyond were more mountains.

Ruby cleared her throat. "I'd like to ask Mrs. Waxler a question, if that's all right with you."

"You're asking permission?" Fargo said.

"I don't want to be gagged."

"Ask it."

Ruby shifted. "It's the same question I asked him. What do you plan to do if you catch up to my friends?"

"I thought I'd made that plain," Geraldine said. "I'm going to kill each and every one of you."

"Just like that?" Ruby scoffed. "When you've never snuffed a wick your whole life?"

"I can do it if I have to," Geraldine said.

"What I don't savvy," Ruby said, glancing at Fargo as if to be sure he didn't mind if she went on talking, "is why you're willing—" She stopped again, her eyes widening in fear.

Fargo wondered why she was looking at him like that. He wasn't doing anything. Then it hit him. She was staring at something *behind* him.

Turning, Fargo started to rise.

An Apache was almost on top of him, a stocky warrior wearing a red headband with a knife in his hand.

The warrior sprang. Fargo got his hand up and seized the man's wrist even as he was slammed onto his back. Iron fingers found his throat, and locked.

The tip of the knife was poised over Fargo's chest. It took all his strength to hold it at bay.

The Apache gouged his fingers deeper, choking off Fargo's breath.

"Don't let him kill you!" Ruby screamed.

Fargo bucked but it had no effect except that the Apache bared his teeth in a wolfish grin. The warrior was confident he would prevail.

Fargo rammed his knee into the Apache's ribs. Once, twice, three times, and the warrior let go and threw himself to one side.

The Apache scrambled into a crouch.

Fargo did the same, but slower. His neck was throbbing. He clawed for his Colt, and discovered his holster was empty. His six-shooter lay a few feet away.

The Apache saw it at the same instant.

Fargo lunged but had to leap back when the warrior slashed at his neck. He backpedaled to gain room and the warrior came after him, his confidence undiminished.

"Do something!" Ruby shrieked.

Fargo wasn't fooled. She was interested only in her own skin. If anything happened to him, the Apache could do whatever he wanted to the women.

Fargo circled, thinking to get close enough to try for his Colt. The Apache, smirking, cut him off.

At the back of Fargo's mind was the worry that the warrior wasn't alone, that others might show up. He dared not look. To take his eyes off the Apache was certain death.

The warrior feinted and came in fast and low, seeking to bury the blade in Fargo's belly. Twisting aside, Fargo saved himself. But only for a moment. The warrior stabbed at his neck. Fargo dodged, and the Apache slashed at his eyes. Again the Apache missed.

Fargo kicked him in the knee. Something snapped, and the Apache grimaced and growled.

The warrior limped a couple of steps, and set himself. Fargo was ready when the warrior's knife sought his chest, and side-stepped. Simultaneously, he landed an uppercut that jarred the warrior onto his heels.

Apaches were deadly fighters but they seldom fought with their fists. Which was why Fargo's next punch, to the warrior's abdomen, wasn't blocked. Fargo cocked his arm to punch again, and a keg of black powder went off between his legs.

Cupping himself, Fargo tried to retreat out of reach but his legs wouldn't work. He tottered, threatening to black out. His blood roared in his ears. Dimly, he was aware of one of the women shrieking a warning. He felt a sharp sting in his chest and braced for the feel of cold steel to be buried in his flesh.

Without warning, Fargo was on his knees. He looked down, expecting to see blood oozing from his wound or the knife hilt jutting from his body. Instead, he saw the Apache on his back, scarlet spurting from a cut that ran from ear to ear.

Over him, holding a bloody knife, was Slits Throats.

"Are you all right?" Geraldine asked.

Fargo nodded. Gradually, his senses returned. That he was alive and unhurt was a miracle.

Slits Throats squatted and began wiping his knife on the dead warrior's breechclout. "You almost die, white-eye."

"How?" Fargo said in confusion. "Where?"

Slits Throats gestured at the dead warrior. "He one of the four."

"What's he doing here?" Fargo said. "I thought they were after the women."

"This one turned back," Slits Throats said. "I not know why but I follow. He come straight here."

"How did he know we were here?" Fargo wondered.

"I not know."

Fargo touched the spot on his shirt where he had felt the sharp sting, and a tiny drop of blood formed on his fingertip. "Damn," he said.

Slits Throats stood and slid his knife into his sheath. "You need eyes like eagle and ears like wolf or you die. Throw Ropes almost had you."

"You know him?" Fargo said.

"Know many Apaches," Slits Throats said. "Chiricahuas, White Mountain, others."

"Yet you killed him to save me?"

"Apache sometimes kill Apache."

"Yes, but . . ." Fargo let it drop. Slits Throats was right. Some of the bands weren't all that friendly. And it wasn't uncommon for an Apache to hire out as an army scout and track down others of his own kind.

"Now you owe me, eh?" Slits Throats said. "Is that not how whites think?"

"I owe you more than I can ever repay."

"Good." Slits Throats smiled. "I maybe find a way."

22

The sunset was beautiful. It blazed a painter's palette of bright colors. Red stood out the most. Not a raspberry red or apple red, but bloodred.

Some people would take that as an omen but Fargo wasn't superstitious. Nor was he much interested in Nature's tapestry. According to Slits Throats, the outlaws weren't more than a quarter of a mile ahead, camped in a hollow.

Fargo was waiting for dark to fall. He'd placed Geraldine and Ruby on either side of a small boulder and looped a rope around them to be doubly certain they didn't go anywhere.

Slits Throats had gone off to watch their quarry and was supposed to report back.

Fargo was impatient to get it over with. If all went well, by morning he'd have corralled the robbers and recovered the money and could head for Fort Bowie. It couldn't happen soon enough to suit him.

"It's nice of you not to gag us tonight," Geraldine remarked. "I sleep better without that rag in my mouth."

Fargo hadn't told them how close they were to the outlaws. It might cause trouble.

"Why didn't you gag us, anyhow?" Ruby asked, suspiciously.

"You won't make any noise," Fargo said.

"How can you be so sure?"

"The only ones likely to hear are the friends of that Apache we killed earlier," Fargo said.

"The last thing I want is for them to find us," Geraldine remarked. "I'm not about to spend the rest of my days in an Apache hovel."

"It wouldn't make much difference to me," Ruby said. "One man is just like another between their legs."

"You're just saying that," Geraldine said. "You wouldn't want to live as a squaw."

"Sister, at this point in my life, I don't much give a damn," Ruby said. "All my life I've catered to men and where did it get me?"

"Men didn't put you up to robbing the payroll."

"No, that was purely my doing," Ruby conceded. "I finally got even for all they put me through."

"Men didn't force you to sell your favors for a living."

"They might as well have," Ruby said. "It's next to impossible for a woman to make ends meet on her own unless she can sew and such. And why? Because men make a hell of a lot more than us women, that's why. Because they control things so we're always second best."

"You could have done like I did and found a good man to marry."

"They're as rare as hen's teeth, and you know it," Ruby said, almost sadly. "It's a fairy tale a lot of gals dream about, but it hardly ever comes true. You were one of the lucky ones."

"And you and your friends killed him."

"I never gave much thought to who we were shooting. I never even looked at their faces. They were obstacles, was all, to us getting our hands on that money."

Fargo turned to look for some sign of Slits Throats and nearly jumped out of his skin. The Apache was close enough to touch. "Where in hell did you come from?"

"I scare you?"

"No."

Slits Throats grinned. "Liar."

"I'm ready to go." Fargo stepped to the Ovaro and slid the Henry from the scabbard. He'd rather rely on the Colt in the dark but if the Apaches did happen by, he could kiss the rifle good-bye.

"Where are you off to?" Geraldine asked.

"To make sure those Apaches aren't anywhere around."

"Why not let the breed do it?" Ruby said.

"Two can cover more ground than one. We won't be long."

"I don't like it," Geraldine said. "Hurry back."

Slits Throats took the lead, moving with a pantherish silence Fargo was hard pressed to match.

The stars were out, their pale glow doing little to relieve the gloom. In due course they climbed to the crest of a ridge and beheld a dancing finger of flame below.

"That them," Slits Throats said.

"What about the Apaches?" Fargo whispered.

"Not see them in a while. Could be anywhere."

"Wonderful."

Warily descending, Fargo avoided loose dirt and rocks. He was eager to get the hunt over with but he couldn't become careless. The women had already shown they were killers.

At the bottom Fargo lost sight of the fire. His unerring sense of direction served him in good stead as he worked his way from cover to cover until muffled voices reached his ear. He crawled the rest of the way.

A woman laughed and others chimed in.

For a pack of murdering she-devils, Fargo reflected, they were in good spirits. He came to a natural bowl over an acre in extent, and there they were.

The fire was small, as it should be. Their horses were tethered in a string and saddled, ready for flight. Another smart move. The women wore revolvers and all had rifles at their sides or across their laps. They had rolled middling-sized boulders to the fire and were seated around it, relaxing.

Another thing Fargo noticed; all four wore riding outfits and riding boots made especially for women. Their hats had wide brims to protect them from the sun. More proof of how well they had planned things.

Three of the women were as ordinary as rainwater. One was a brunette, another a redhead, the third had hair the color of caramel, cut so short it was mannish.

The last one had to be Big Bertha. She was as wide as a buckboard, practically, with great rolling shoulders and legs like tree stumps. She had a deep voice, and a booming peal of a laugh that

made her whole body shake. Her face was a moon with freak-
ishly big eyes, her jowls sagged like extra chins, and her nose was
twice the size it should have been.

Fargo couldn't quite hear what they were saying. Taking a
gamble, he slid over the edge. A few pebbles rattled, and he froze.

The redhead glanced in his direction. "Hold on," she said.
"Did any of you hear that?"

"What?" Big Bertha rumbled.

"I don't know. Something."

"Go have a look, Claire."

The redhead snatched her rifle and rose. She walked with an
exaggerated sway of her hips, as many doves did, but she was as
grim as death.

Fargo hugged the ground, hoping she wouldn't spot him. He'd
like to avoid shooting them if he could help it, although there
were plenty of folks who'd say they had it coming.

"Anything?" the brunette called out when Claire was halfway.

"Nothing yet, Theresa."

The woman with the short hair stood. "Want me to come
help?"

"Stay put, Alvena," Big Bertha said.

Fargo fixed a bead on Claire. She was between him and the
fire, and he had a perfect shot at her silhouette. She took a couple
more steps, and stopped.

"I don't see anyone."

"Come on back, then," Big Bertha said.

"I thought it might be Ruby," Claire said, shouldering her
rifle. "She should have been back by now."

"If she hasn't shown by morning, we'll go find her," Big Bertha said. "Remember my rule."

"Which one?" Theresa said. "You have a hundred."

"They've kept us alive, haven't they?" Big Bertha said. "And
the rule I mean is that we don't leave anyone behind. We all make
it back or none of us do."

"I should have gone with her," Alvena said.

Fargo resumed his descent. He would get as close as he could
before springing his surprise.

Claire claimed her boulder and leaned her rifle against her
leg. "I still can't get over how easy it's been."

"I wouldn't go that far," Theresa said.

"We cut those troopers down without any of us being so much
as nicked," Claire said. "We loaded the money and got out of

there so fast, we were long gone before the army got there. And we have enough water and grub to last us until we reach Tucson."

"Planning, girls," Big Bertha said. "I planned this out to the smallest detail."

"Don't forget all the practice you put us through," Alvena said. "All that shooting and riding."

"More of my planning," Big Bertha said.

"You made a believer out of me," Claire complimented her.

Theresa took off her hat and set it on her knee. "I won't rest easy until we've split the money and scattered to the four winds."

"You worry too much," Big Bertha said. "You always have."

Fargo reached a boulder and rose to his knee. He'd lost track of Slits Throats. It was up to him to start things rolling, preferably without being shot.

"It's a shame no one will ever know it was us," Alvena said. "We'd be plumb famous."

"For robbing some soldiers?" Claire said, and laughed.

"I'm serious," Alvena said. "Name another woman who's done what we did? Hell, for that matter, name a man."

"Shooting folks isn't anything special," Claire said. "People do it all the time."

Raising the Henry, Fargo rested it on the boulder. He had clear shots at all four. Only then did he spy the pile of money bags near Big Bertha. One was open and several coins had spilled out.

"It's San Francisco for me," Theresa was saying. "As far away as I can get without leaving the country."

"I'm partial to Florida," Alvena said. "I have an aunt who lives there and she makes it sound like paradise."

"How about you, Bertha?" Claire asked. "You haven't told us where you aim to go."

"And I never will," Big Bertha responded. "Any of you get caught, you could set the law on me."

"We'd never do that," Alvena said.

Fargo was ready. Curling back the hammer, he yelled, "Ladies! Throw down your guns and put your hands in the air."

23

The three younger women—Claire, Theresa, and Alvena—whipped their heads around, startled. But the mountain called Big Bertha fixed her dark eyes on Fargo with no more concern than if he were a lizard. She didn't seem the least surprised. "Well, well, well," she rumbled.

"Your hands in the air," Fargo commanded. "Don't make me shoot you."

"Foolish man," Big Bertha said, and then, louder, "You know what to do, girls. What are you waiting for?"

Claire, Theresa, and Alvena burst into motion, each snatching her rifle and darting into the darkness.

Fargo had time only to aim at Alvena but he didn't shoot. Her back was to him, and he couldn't bring himself to squeeze the trigger.

The women had no such compunctions.

The night abruptly rocked with thunder as all three started shooting in his direction. Each had a repeater. Their hail of lead sizzled the air and struck the boulder Fargo was behind.

Dropping flat, Fargo sought a target. There was no one to shoot except Bertha, who hadn't moved. He aimed at her and hollered, "Tell them to throw down their rifles and show themselves or I'll shoot you."

"Shoot me," Bertha said.

"I'm not bluffing," Fargo said.

"Me, either."

Damned if she wasn't serious, Fargo realized. He centered on her chest and hesitated. All she had in her hands was a tin cup. "I don't have to kill you," he shouted. "I can shoot you in the leg."

"Do it," Big Bertha said. "Or don't you have the gumption?" Her broad face crinkled in contempt.

Fargo had blundered. He'd taken it for granted the women would do as he wanted, that taking them into custody would be simple. He hadn't counted on anything like this. They didn't act like ordinary women. They acted more like trained soldiers.

As if to drive that point home, a rifle spanged and a geyser of dirt erupted in his face. One of them had changed position. He figured the rest would, too. They'd come at him from three sides and catch him in a cross fire.

"Hell," Fargo muttered, and slid backward.

Another shot cracked.

Fargo returned fire, rolled, and heaved into a crouch. Whirling, he sped for the rim, zigzagging in case they opened up on him, which they did, half a dozen shots that peppered his vicinity. They were good shots.

Weaving and scrambling, Fargo reached the top and glanced back.

Big Bertha still hadn't moved. She still held her cup in both hands and was taking a sip.

Figures flitted toward him, patches of moving ink. A firefly flared and a slug kicked earth at his feet.

Fargo got out of there. He could have stayed and made a fight of it but they outnumbered him and their rifles more than matched his own. Or was he making excuses? he asked himself as he ran. Was he reluctant to do what needed doing because they were women? If they were men, would he tuck tail?

No, Fargo told himself. He probably wouldn't.

He didn't stop. He checked behind often but the women hadn't given chase.

He'd covered over half the distance to where he'd left Geraldine and Ruby when a loping shape materialized almost at his side. Digging in his bootheels, he snapped, "Where the hell did you get to?"

"I stay close," Slits Throats said. "I see what you do."

"You didn't do anything."

"I say I help you find women. I not say I help you fight them."

"Well, hell," Fargo said, and continued on. The warrior had been true to his word. He couldn't fault him there.

Slits Throats fell in beside him. "They make you run," he said, and his teeth were white in the darkness.

"I don't want to kill them if I can help it."

"Why not?" Slits Throats asked. "They killed blue coats."

"It's not how whites do things," Fargo said.

"Not eye for eye?"

Fargo wondered where he'd heard that. "They should be put on trial. Go before a judge."

"Apache way better. Anyone who is enemy, Apache kill. No trial. No judge."

"They're white women," Fargo said. "They have to answer to white justice."

"If that how you want it," Slits Throats said, his tone suggesting it was the stupidest thing he'd ever heard.

Geraldine and Ruby were sitting with their heads hung in resignation. Both stiffened when they heard his footsteps.

"There you are," Geraldine said, sounding relieved. "I was worried something had happened to you."

"And you'd be stuck tied to that boulder and starve to death or die of thirst," Fargo said.

"There were shots," Ruby said, "far off."

"Your friends."

"We've caught up to them?" Ruby peered into the night as if she thought she might see them. "I figured they'd be farther ahead."

"They won't leave without you," Fargo informed her.

A flush spread up Ruby's face, and she gave a little smile. "Well, now. She's as good as her word, Bertha is."

"Who?" Geraldine said.

"Bertha Gugelgeist," Ruby answered. "Or as all the doves who worked for her called her, Big Bertha."

Geraldine went rigid. "No!" she exclaimed.

"What's the matter?" Fargo said.

Ruby, looking over her shoulder at Geraldine, laughed. "You're finally figuring it out? It took you long enough."

"Figured what out?" Fargo said. He suddenly realized Slits Throats wasn't there. Once again, the warrior had disappeared.

"Bertha Gugelgeist," Geraldine said. "I thought she was a friend."

Fargo tore his gaze from the chaparral. "You *know* her?"

"I worked for her. She ran the sporting house where I met Hank. He got along great with her. We even invited her to our wedding."

"The hell you say."

"How could she have killed him and his men?" Geraldine said, aghast.

Fargo pondered, a suspicion taking root. "Did Bertha know Hank was with the paymaster office?"

"Come to think of it," Geraldine said slowly, "I remember her asking a lot of questions about his job. Are you suggesting . . . ?"

"Slow as molasses," Ruby said.

"He told her it was his job to deliver pay to the forts," Fargo guessed. "Somehow she found out about his latest run, and ambushed them." Although there had to be more to it than that. Based on what he'd overheard, Bertha and her gang had practiced for weeks if not months to prepare for the robbery.

"But how could they have known?" Geraldine said.

Ruby snorted. "How dumb are you? It's easy for one of us to get a soldier to talk. Ply them with coffin varnish and take them to bed and they'll spill their life's story."

"Oh God." Geraldine closed her eyes and bowed her head.

"Go ahead and cry," Ruby said. "It serves you right for being so stupid."

Jerking her head up, Geraldine twisted and glared. "How could she murder my husband after he was so nice to her?"

"She did you a favor, if you ask me," Ruby said. "Men are as worthless as teats on a boar."

Tears of rage filled Geraldine's eyes and she struggled fiercely against her bounds. "Let me loose. Let me at her."

"Calm down," Fargo said.

"I'll rip your eyes out, bitch," Geraldine raged.

All Ruby did was laugh.

Fargo went around the boulder and squatted in front of Geraldine, who was doing her utmost to free herself. "Listen to me."

"I want her dead—you hear me? I want all of them dead. Bertha most of all."

Fargo placed a hand on her shoulder. "You're forgetting something."

"I haven't forgotten a damn thing," Geraldine said, straining.

"The Apaches who have been stalking Bertha's bunch," Fargo reminded her. "Do you want them to hear you?"

That gave her pause.

"They might come see what the ruckus is about."

Geraldine slowly relaxed. "I still want them dead. More than ever."

"I don't blame you." Rising, Fargo went around to the other side. "I'd like to hear more about the rifle practice and riding Bertha made you do."

"Go to hell," Ruby said with mock sweetness.

"What harm can it do?"

Ruby's brow furrowed. "None, I suppose. Yes, she put us through six weeks of training so the robbery would go off without a hitch.

Evenings and Sundays, she drilled us as if we were soldiers. She bought us all Henrys and we learned to use them. We rode horses until our behinds were sore. We even practiced things like kindling a fire and how to tell direction by the stars."

"Sounds like she didn't miss a thing," Fargo said.

"Not Bertha. She's smart, that lady. She ran her sporting house the same way. Like a finely tuned watch, was how she put it. She was always saying that if we got the small things right, the big things would work themselves out."

"It didn't bother any of them, having to kill those troopers?"

Ruby shrugged. "I told you before. All we cared about was the money."

Disgusted, Fargo turned away . . . and found himself staring into the muzzle of a rifle.

24

"Remember us?" the woman called Claire said, and thumbed back the hammer.

The other two materialized out of the gloom, both with their own rifles trained.

"I bet he does," Alvena said, grinning. "You don't forget someone who tried to kill you."

"If at first we don't succeed . . ." Theresa said, and laughed.

Ruby sat frozen with delight for all of five seconds, then let out a squeal. "Sisters! I can't tell you how happy you've just made me."

Fargo stayed still as Alvena came around and relieved him of his Henry and the Colt.

Theresa drew a knife to free Ruby.

As for Claire, she lowered her rifle's muzzle close to his crotch. "So much as twitch and you can say good-bye to your pecker."

Fargo was puzzled that they hadn't shot him where he stood. "Why am I still alive?"

"Are you complaining?" Alvena said.

"You're alive," Claire said, "because Big Bertha told us to bring you back breathing if we could. She wants to have words with you."

"Lucky you," Alvena said.

Fargo had no choice but to go along with them for the time being, and wait for them to become careless.

Ruby had risen and was rubbing her wrists. "My arms are tingling so bad, it hurts." She took a step toward Fargo. "Trussing me like a piglet for slaughter. I should gut you."

"You heard me say Big Bertha wants to talk to him," Claire said.

Theresa was studying Geraldine. "Who's this? Do I cut her free, too?"

"You don't recognize her?" Ruby said.

"I've never set eyes on her before," Theresa said.

"It's the paymaster's missus," Ruby said. "The whore who thought she'd made good."

"No fooling?" Theresa said. To Geraldine she said, "How's it feel to have gotten your husband killed?"

"Me?" Geraldine said.

"It was through you that Bertha met him. Through you she found out what he did for a living. Through you she got her brain-storm."

"Shoot her," Alvena said.

"No." From Claire. "Bertha might want to talk to her, too. We'll take them both, and their horses."

"Where's the breed?" Ruby asked.

The other three looked at her quizzically.

"He's been helping track you," Ruby enlightened them. "Answers to the handle of Slits Throats."

"Never saw any breed," Claire said. "Only this scout, here."

"We'd best get back then," Alvena said. "And stick close together."

Theresa hauled Geraldine to her feet and cut her legs free so she could walk. Giving her a push, she jabbed her rifle against Geraldine's spine. "Behave and you'll live a little longer."

Alvena brought the horses.

At gunpoint, Fargo was marched toward the hollow. This was what he got for going easy on them earlier, he reflected. Everything had gone to hell. "What does Bertha want to talk to me about?"

"How would I know?" Claire said. "Hush and walk."

Fargo wondered if Slits Throats would come to his aid. He doubted it. A hard poke in his back spurred him into saying, "Go easy with that thing."

"You don't give the orders here," Claire said. "No man ever tells me what to do ever again."

"Hear, hear," Ruby said.

"Doves who don't like men," Fargo said. "That's a new one."

"What do you know?" Claire said. "All our lives, women have been nothing but glorified servants to you men. Women cook for men, we darn their socks, and we keep them warm at night, and what does it get us?"

"Men keep women warm, too."

"That's not the point," Claire said. "It figures you don't understand. Typical damn man."

"Bertha will set him straight," Theresa said. "She's good at making people see the light."

"There's a light now?" Fargo said. "Is it a lamp or a lantern or what?"

"Ha, ha," Claire said. "Now shut the hell up."

Fargo was tempted to bolt. If he moved fast enough, if she missed with her first shot, if he could find cover, he might get away. That was a lot of "ifs" though. He trudged along until they reached the hollow.

Big Bertha hadn't moved. She was still drinking coffee. Smiling as they approached, she said, "Well done, girls. You make me proud."

Before anyone could hope to stop her, Geraldine Waxler shoved Theresa and barreled around the fire, her fists balled. "You despicable wretch!" she screamed, and threw herself at the larger woman.

"Bertha!" Alvena cried.

She needn't have worried.

With a quickness that belied her bulk, Big Bertha backhanded Geraldine across the face. The sharp *crack* of the blow jolted Geraldine onto her heels. Bertha's foot rose, catching Geraldine in the knee, and Geraldine uttered a different kind of scream as she staggered and stumbled and fell.

"That ought to teach you," Big Bertha said.

"That's our Bertha," Ruby proudly declared, and she and the others laughed.

Geraldine was clutching her leg and rolling back and forth,

her features contorted in anguish. "Bitch!" she hissed. "I thought you were my friend."

"I came to your wedding, didn't I?" Bertha said. "And I thank you, again, for the invite. That's where I first got the idea to steal a payroll. Your husband mentioned that he often delivered payrolls worth more than twenty thousand dollars. That got me to thinking."

Geraldine managed to sit up. "*That's* when you decided you would kill him? At my wedding?"

"You're not listening. It was his mention of all that money. I already knew he went around delivering to army posts. I just never imagined it was so much."

"My own wedding," Geraldine said again.

"After that I started to keep track of him. Made it a point to have my girls question the troopers that worked for him. Bit by bit I came up with a plan to put me on easy street for the rest of my born days."

Fargo was being ignored. All eyes were on Bertha and Geraldine. Acting casual, he glanced at the Ovaro. Alvena had let go of the reins and moved up beside Theresa. Gauging the distance, he tensed. It was worth the try.

Uncannily, Big Bertha picked that moment to turn toward him. "You're a scout, I take it."

"His name is Skye Fargo," Ruby said.

Big Bertha tilted her head. "Heard of you. Heard that you're one of the best scouts around. Also heard that you can't keep your pecker in your pants."

"That pretty much sums me up," Fargo said.

"The colonel at Fort Bowie set you on our trail, I expect," Big Bertha said.

"Only doing my job," Fargo told her.

"Just you and no soldiers? He must think highly of you."

Fargo didn't mention to her he'd refused the help.

Bertha indicated an empty boulder. "Have a seat. I need to know a few things and you're going to tell me."

Claire and Theresa stepped forward to cover him.

"Whatever you want," Fargo said, and roosted. He still had his toothpick but if he drew it, he'd be blasted before he could use it.

"I have a hard time believing you're by your lonesome," Bertha said. "The colonel and his blue-bellies must be following you."

No, they weren't, but it gave Fargo an idea. "No use in lying," he lied. "I came on ahead alone and have been leaving markers for them to follow."

"I knew it," Big Bertha said. "How far behind are they?"

"I don't know."

"It would be a mistake to take me for a fool."

"I honestly don't," Fargo said. "It depends on how long it took Colonel Chivington to get his men ready, and how hard they've been pushing. If I had to guess, I'd say they're probably a day or two behind me."

"It could be less, though," Big Bertha said. "A lot less."

"If you don't believe me, send one of your girls and find out," Fargo said. He was looking at the Ovaro, not at her, and didn't see her hand move. He felt the blow, though. He was sent sprawling in the dirt, his ears ringing from the force of it.

"I don't like your tone."

Fargo would have jumped her, female or no, but Claire and Ruby were sighting down their barrels.

"How many soldiers are there? Be exact."

Fargo said the first number that popped into his head. "Twenty-eight."

"That many?" Claire said.

"The colonel's not going to send a handful and have them wiped out like the major and his men," Big Bertha said.

"You also have Apaches after you," Fargo said, hoping to rattle them so they'd make a mistake and he could reach the Ovaro.

"We haven't seen any," Bertha said, and rising, she stood over him with her hands on her hips.

"Ask Ruby," Fargo said.

"I don't need to," Big Bertha said. "Apaches don't scare me none."

Fargo should have kept his mouth shut but didn't. "Then you're not as smart as you think you are. They scare anyone with half a brain."

"Is that a fact?" Big Bertha said. "But let's back up a bit. You told me there are twenty-eight troopers. How would you know that unless you left the same time they did? Which means you lied about being sent on ahead."

"I didn't think of that," Theresa said.

"He must have been lying," Alvena agreed.

"And I do so despise liars," Big Bertha said. "I think you need to be taught a lesson, scout." And with that, she rammed into him.

25

A foot bigger than his own swept at Fargo. He rolled to keep from having his face kicked in and kept on rolling, putting distance between them.

Big Bertha came after him. She was surprisingly nimble. She caught him in the side, sending pain through his ribs, and then did a remarkable thing; she jumped into the air and bent her knees to come down on top of him like an avalanche.

Fargo flung himself away. He heard the thud of her hitting the ground, and then a hand with fingers as thick as spikes wrapped around his arm. He tried to tear free but she was incredibly strong. A fist grazed his cheek. He retaliated with a right cross to the jaw that would have rocked most men. She didn't even blink.

The other lady outlaws were hollering encouragement, shouting for her to pound him into the dirt, as Claire put it, or to bust his skull open, as Ruby wanted.

It was galling enough that Big Bertha had attacked him. It was doubly so that she was smiling as if it amused her.

Fargo whipped a roundhouse to her face but Bertha blocked it. Suddenly she was on top of him, straddling him. It was like being straddled by a ten-ton boulder.

"This is going to hurt," Big Bertha sneered. "A lot."

Fargo's arms and chest were pinned but his legs were free. He arced his knees, slamming them into her back. It was like hitting a sack of flour. But Bertha grimaced, which encouraged him to do it several more times.

Big Bertha's sneer became a scowl. "Nice try," she said.

Extending his legs, Fargo swung them up as high as they would go. He hoped to kick her in the back of her head; his boots connected with her neck.

Bertha growled like a mad she-bear. Releasing his left wrist, she drove her fist at his face.

Fargo twisted, but she clipped him on the jaw. And damn, she could punch.

"Hit him again!" Alvena cried.

"Hurt him bad!" Ruby yelled.

Fargo struck Bertha on the cheek, on the neck. Neither had an effect.

The next moment a gun blasted.

Big Bertha looked up in alarm, bawling, "Who's shooting?"

Fargo, like Bertha, figured it was one of the women. But a second shot proved otherwise.

"It's someone off in the dark!" Claire cried.

Big Bertha heaved off Fargo and clawed for the revolver on her hip. "Get down! Take cover!"

Fargo pushed to his hands and knees as all of them began shooting wildly into the night. He spied his Henry and Colt by the fire and in two bounds reached them. Scooping them up, he didn't stop. He was out of the firelight when several shots were sent his way.

Weaving, he ran faster.

Only when he was out of the hollow and had gone another fifty yards did Fargo come to a halt.

The gunshots were tapering off. Big Bertha was bellowing something but he couldn't catch the words.

Catching his breath, Fargo shoved the Colt into his holster and patted the Henry. He had half a mind to do some shooting of his own.

Hooves humped and Slits Throats walked up as casually as you please, leading the Ovaro and the bay by the reins.

"I should have known," Fargo said.

"They busy with you, I take horses."

"You pulled my bacon out of the fire," Fargo said by way of gratitude. "I'm obliged."

"You die, white-eye, I not get hundred dollars." Slits Throats held out the Ovaro's reins. "Want help climbing on?"

"Help?" Fargo said.

"I saw big woman attack you."

"Don't remind me."

"You being beat"—Slits Throats smirked—"by a woman."

"She might be female but she's as tough as any man I ever tangled with," Fargo said.

"That good excuse," Slits Throats said.

"You think this is funny, do you?"

Turning, Slits Throats swung onto the bay. "Good thing other women not help her. You be beaten to pulp by now."

"I'd like to have seen you do any better," Fargo said as he shoved the Henry into the scabbard.

"Apache not fight women," Slits Throats said. "Apache shoot them."

Forking leather, Fargo reined to the east. The bay came alongside but he stared straight ahead.

"Maybe I ask for more money," Slits Throats said. "Fifty dollars each time I save you."

"That was the last time you'll need to," Fargo promised himself.

"You want advice?"

"No."

"You too easy on them."

The hell of it was, Fargo reflected, his new partner was right. If those women were men, he'd have shot some by now.

"White men always too easy on women. It why your women soft and not good for much."

Fargo clucked to the Ovaro, and Slits Throats took the hint and dropped behind him, chuckling.

It wasn't long before a dry wash unfolded before them. Going down in, Fargo drew rein. "We'll rest here for the night," he announced.

Stripping their horses, they settled in. Fargo spread out his bedroll and cupped his hands under his head for a pillow.

Splits Throats curled on his side on the ground and was soon asleep.

For Fargo, it proved more elusive. He couldn't stop thinking of Geraldine, and what Big Bertha and the others might do to her. By rights, he shouldn't give a damn; Geraldine had left him bound and helpless for Slits Throats to kill. But he would save her if he could.

To complicate things, there were the Apaches who were shadowing the women. Most likely, the warriors were after their weapons and their horses. The warriors could be anywhere.

There seemed to Fargo to be only one thing to do. He must stop holding back. He must corral the women, or do whatever was necessary if they resisted, and head for Fort Bowie.

His mind made up, he drifted off. He slept soundly and awoke at his usual time, the crack of dawn. Sitting up, he stretched and turned to Slits Throats, only the half-breed wasn't there. The bay was, though, so Fargo reckoned the warrior hadn't gone far.

He didn't bother with coffee. Rolling up his bedroll, he saddled the Ovaro and was ready to head out as soon as Slits Throats returned.

To the east, the sky became bright with the molten hues of the new day.

Fargo became restless. Slits Throats was taking too long. He climbed to the top of the wash and scoured the plain and the hills and mountains all around. There was no sign of him.

By now Big Bertha and her gang of fallen doves were up and under way.

Fargo couldn't wait around much longer.

Just when he was about to climb on the Ovaro, a figure appeared, loping at a tireless dogtrot.

"About time," Fargo grumbled to himself. He impatiently waited, and when Slits Throats reached him, demanded, "Where in blazes have you been? We should have headed out an hour ago."

Unruffled, Slits Throats replied, "I hunt for Apaches."

"And?"

"No sign."

"Then what are we waiting for?" Climbing on the Ovaro, Fargo rode up out of the wash. In the cool of early morning he had no qualms about bringing the stallion to a trot.

He glanced back several times but Slits Throats didn't appear.

Fargo wasn't about to go back to find out why. The warrior could take care of himself.

As he neared the hollow, Fargo palmed his Colt. He didn't expect to find the women there, and they weren't. The charred embers of their fire were all that remained.

Circling, Fargo found where their tracks pointed to the northwest. They'd ridden in single file, the packhorses at the rear.

Fargo checked an urge to spur the Ovaro to a gallop. The temperature was rising.

By midday it would be over a hundred.

Judging by the tracks, Bertha and company were pushing harder than before. Their only hope of getting away lay in reaching Tucson and scattering to parts unknown.

Mile after mile fell behind him.

A lizard sunning itself skittered away. A hawk looked him over and winged elsewhere.

By noon Fargo's throat was parched but he didn't touch his canteen. He thought about that tank he knew of. If the women kept on the way they were, he wouldn't pass anywhere near it.

Along about one o'clock, Fargo happened to glance to his left and almost drew rein in surprise. A lone rider was pacing him far off. Distorted by the heat haze, the man and his mount were little more than moving sticks.

The horse appeared to be a bay. It must be Slits Throats, Fargo reckoned. But why he was so far off was a mystery.

Not five minutes later Fargo looked to his right and his gut balled into a knot.

Another rider was pacing him about the same distance as the first.

"Two of them," Fargo said aloud. Shifting in the saddle, he swore.

A third rider, well out of rifle range but closer than the other two, left no doubt as to who they were. This one wore a headband and moccasins and held a rifle with the stock on his thigh.

Fargo shrugged off a ripple of unease.

The three Apaches who had been shadowing the women were now shadowing him.

Just then the pair on either side began to close in.

26

Fargo wasn't surprised the Apaches were being so blatant about it. As cats often did with mice, Apaches sometimes liked to toy with their prey.

The pair on his flanks didn't come within range of his Henry. They were too smart for that.

Fargo wondered if they knew that the fourth member of their

little war party was dead, and they were out to repay the favor. In that case they might want to take him alive so they could make him suffer.

For the better part of an hour nothing changed. Then, on an impulse, Fargo reined toward the warrior on the right. The warrior immediately reined away to keep the same distance between them. When Fargo reined back again, so did the Apache.

Ahead reared another mountain range, the foremost slope was crowned by low cliffs.

From up there, Fargo mused, he could hold the warriors off a good long while.

A series of switchbacks led up to the cliffs, the bottom of the first littered with talus.

Fargo swung wide to avoid it. The last thing he needed was for the stallion to break a leg, or worse.

A flash of light caused him to draw rein. The sun had reflected off metal, he suspected. It could be a rifle barrel. He rose in the stirrups but the flash wasn't repeated.

The Apaches had stopped, too.

Sliding the Henry out, Fargo levered a cartridge into the chamber. He started up, hunched over his saddle.

The Apaches sat and watched.

Fargo raked the high slopes for anything out of the ordinary, but nothing.

Suddenly raising its head, the stallion pricked its ears.

Fargo was in a bind. Someone was above him, Apaches were on either side and behind him. He was in the open, exposed, easy pickings. And every instinct he possessed was screaming at him to get out of there.

He did.

Hauling on the reins, Fargo flew toward a manzanita fifty feet away. It wasn't much cover but it was better than nothing. He tapped his spurs just as a rifle cracked, high up. He felt a tug on his hat but it stayed on his head.

Another rifle opened up, and a third. But he was moving so fast, they missed.

Fargo avoided a boulder, clattered across a stretch of pebbles, and brought the Ovaro to a stop behind the manzanita. Vaulting down, he sank to his knees and craned his neck to see the upper slopes.

The women had stopped firing.

Momentarily safe, Fargo turned. The Apaches on either side

116

were no longer there. He looked behind him. The third one had disappeared, too.

"Damn."

Fargo settled down to wait. The women wouldn't stay up there forever. Eventually they would move on, and so would he.

About twenty minutes had gone by when a rider materialized up near the cliffs and descended toward him. Her size left no doubt as to who it was. Taking her sweet time, she worked her way down the switchbacks until she was within earshot of the manzanita.

"That's far enough," Fargo said.

"We need to talk," Big Bertha hollered.

"I'm listening," Fargo replied, without showing himself.

"Face-to-face," Big Bertha said. "It's important."

Wondering what she was up to, Fargo called out, "Come ahead. But keep your hands where I can see them."

Bertha held her palms out. "Don't you worry. I'm not looking to get myself shot. All I want is to have words. I promise."

Fargo covered her as she came around the manzanita and reined up. "Let me hear what you have to say."

Leaning on her saddle horn, Big Bertha wiped her sleeve across her sweaty neck. "You have more lives than a cat—do you know that?"

"*That's* what you came down to tell me?"

"Be serious," Bertha said.

"What are you doing here, then?"

"I came to ask you to give up."

Fargo stared in amazement. He could tell she was serious. "Has the sun baked your brains?"

"Last night you claimed I don't have any," Bertha said. "But tell me. Do you gamble much? Cards and the like?"

"Every chance I get," Fargo said. His fondness for poker was second only to his fondness for a willing vixen.

"Not me. I never take chances when I don't have to. Take now, for instance. You probably think I took a big chance riding down here like this. But the truth is, I have an ace up my sleeve that you can't beat."

"I must have missed it," Fargo said.

"You're the one who brought it to me," Big Bertha said. "Or should I say, her."

"Geraldine Waxler?"

"The very same," Bertha said. "I would have shot her last

117

night but I held on to her in case you showed up so I could use her to bargain with."

"She's nothing to me."

"I believe you," Bertha said. "Ruby has told me that you and Geraldine don't get along. But that's neither here nor there. What matters is that she stays alive only if you do exactly as I say."

Fargo glanced up the mountain. He should have expected something like this. "You are a work of art."

"Now, now," Big Bertha said. "We work with what we have, and I have her. Or, rather, my girls do, up yonder. Which brings us to Ruby again."

"This should be good." Fargo knew what was coming but couldn't think of a way to thwart it.

"You're not the only one who can't get along with Geraldine. Ruby hates her guts. They've had some disagreements, I understand, and Ruby would like nothing better than to put her rifle to Geraldine's temple and squeeze the trigger."

"Ruby's a regular sweetheart," Fargo said.

"Is that any way to talk about a gal who let you poke her?"

"She told you about that?"

"My girls tell me everything," Bertha boasted. "She said that you should have your very own stud farm."

"I aim to please," Fargo said.

"Then hand me that rifle and your six-shooter," Big Bertha commanded. "Or the next shot you hear will be Ruby splattering Geraldine Waxler's brains."

"I give you my guns and my own brains will be splattered."

"What if I give you my word they won't be? What if I promise to let you and Geraldine go. Take her and your horses and light a shuck."

"Just like that?" Fargo said, snapping his fingers.

"You did hear the part about turning over your artillery?" Bertha said. "You're no threat to us without them."

"Speaking of threats," Fargo said. "Those three Apaches are dogging us. You must have seen them."

"I did, indeed," Bertha said.

"And you expect me to try and make it past them with nothing to fight with except harsh language?"

"If you use your wits you can do it."

"I have a better idea," Fargo said.

"I warn you. Don't try anything. Ruby will kill Geraldine if you do. All I have to do is raise my arm and Waxler joins her precious husband in the hereafter."

"That works both ways," Fargo said.

"How do you mean?"

"You raise your arm, Ruby shoots Geraldine, and I shoot you. So go ahead. Raise it."

Bertha wasn't fazed. "You're bluffing. You had your chance to shoot me last night and you didn't."

"I try not to make the same mistake twice," Fargo said, and aimed the Henry.

"Now you just hold on," Bertha said, showing concern for the first time. "I came down here in good faith to parley."

"To threaten, is more like it," Fargo said. "And to gloat and rub my nose in it once you got the better of me."

"You're a man," Bertha said. "You deserve what you get."

"We're back to that again," Fargo said. It occurred to Fargo she might be stalling, that perhaps she wasn't alone, that one of the others might be sneaking up on him as they spoke.

"We never left it," Bertha said. "I'm sick to death of men, of them lording it over us women. If I could find somewhere in this world there aren't any males, I'd be the happiest person alive."

"It will make me happy if you climb down and bring your horse over here."

Bertha locked eyes with him. She was taking his measure, and she must not have liked what she saw because she slipped her right foot from the stirrup and alighted with as much dignity as she could muster. "Geraldine Waxler is as good as dead."

"Is that so?" Fargo moved to where he could see the higher slopes. Up near the cliffs there was another flash, but no shot. Cupping his left hand to his mouth, he shouted, "If you can hear me up there, send someone else down to talk."

"What are you up to?" Big Bertha asked.

"You have ten minutes," Fargo hollered.

"No one will come," Bertha said. "None of my girls are that dumb."

"For you they will." Fargo crooked a finger. "Why are you still standing here?"

Her lip twitching, Bertha led her mount over. "Happy now?"

"Not quite." Holding the Henry steady on her face, Fargo relieved her of her revolver and her rifle and motioned for her to follow him around the manzanita where he tossed her weapons to the ground.

119

"Enjoy this while you can," Bertha said.

Fargo was too tense to enjoy anything. He didn't dare turn his back on her, and the Apaches were still around.

"I'll be damned," Bertha declared. She was looking up the mountain.

Another woman was on her way down.

"I told you," Fargo said.

Big Bertha looked fit to tear into him. "So you were right. So what? It doesn't change the fact that before this is done, we're going to put you under."

27

The woman coming down the mountain was Claire. She held her rifle across her saddle, and by her posture, she was ready to use it in an instant if she had to.

Fargo held up his hand when she was close enough to hear him. "That's far enough," he said. He kept his Henry trained on Bertha.

Claire drew rein. She looked worriedly at Big Bertha and asked, "Are you all right? Has he hurt you?"

Instead of answering, Bertha said, "Why didn't I hear a shot? Why didn't you kill the Waxler woman like you were supposed to?"

"He has you," Claire said.

"So?" Bertha said angrily. "What does it take to get through those thick heads of yours? You're to do as I say. At all times."

"We were worried that if we shot Geraldine, he'd shoot you."

Big Bertha sighed in disappointment. "I try and I try and you still don't listen. I told you girls from the beginning. For this to work we have to do what needs doing whether we like it or not."

"We won't let you be harmed," Claire said.

"Enough," Fargo said.

Claire finally seemed to notice him. "Why did you want one of us to come down here?"

"To set up a swap," Fargo said. "Bring Geraldine Waxler to me and you can have Bertha."

"Why do you care what happens to her? Ruby told us she tried to have you killed."

How could Fargo explain? Sure, if all he was interested in was an eye for an eye, then he should leave Geraldine to her fate. But that wasn't in his nature. He would do what he could to save her. "Do we have a deal or not?"

Big Bertha spoke first. "Don't do it, Claire. Tell the others I said they're not to trade her no matter what. You hear me?"

"What if we don't trade?" Claire asked Fargo.

"I'll hand Bertha over to the army and let them know about the rest of you. Your names. What you look like. Federal marshals will be brought in to track you down. They might even hire the Pinkertons," Fargo said. All of which was true except that last.

"The Pinkertons?" Claire said. "I hear they never give up. When they take a case, they hunt and they hunt until they find who they're after."

"I've heard the same thing," Fargo said.

"What if we don't hand Waxler over?" Claire asked. "What will you do then?"

"I'll take Bertha to Fort Bowie and tell the army all about you. Once she's behind bars, I'll come after you myself."

"I don't want that," Claire said. "You've been like a wolf on the scent of a deer. You don't know when to quit."

"You're not to trade me, damn it," Big Bertha said. "I'll be mad as hell and terribly disappointed if you do."

Fargo could tell Claire was wavering. "Go and talk to the others. Ask what they want to do. Take a vote. I'll keep Bertha here until you decide."

"There's nothing to decide," Bertha said.

Claire gnawed on her lip.

"Damn it, girl," Big Bertha said. "You're not to swap that prissy bitch for me. You hear me?"

"I'll talk it over with the others," Claire told Fargo.

"Like hell you will," Big Bertha said.

Claire raised her reins and said to her, "I'm sorry, Bertha. I know we're supposed to do as you tell us. But we won't let anything happen to you if we can help it, no matter what."

"I'm not important," Big Bertha said. "The money is."

"What good is the money if we're not all alive to spend it?" Claire argued, and wheeled her mount.

"Don't take too long," Fargo said. He was worried about those Apaches. They could be anywhere.

Claire nodded and slapped her legs.

"Damn it all," Big Bertha grumbled, watching her ride off. "They're not going to listen. They're going to swap me. And after all the hours and days and weeks I spent getting it through their thick heads to listen to me."

"You should be flattered they care," Fargo said.

"What do you know?" Bertha shot back. "They should shoot that cretin, take the money, and go. That's the smart thing, and I've said all along that we have to do this smart. Feelings don't enter into it. We let sentiment cloud our judgment, we're in for trouble."

Fargo moved into the scant shade of the manzanita and squatted. "Make yourself comfortable."

Her jaw muscles clenching, Big Bertha sat with her back to the bole. "Just so you know, if I ever get my hands on you . . ." She didn't finish.

"Just so *you* know," Fargo said, "I'm through going easy on you. From here on out, I treat you the same as I'd treat a gang of men."

"Thank you," Bertha said.

Fargo arched an eyebrow.

"You still don't savvy, do you? What do you think this has been about?" Big Bertha paused. "We're tired of men lording it over us. Of treating us as if they're our betters. We want to be treated with the same respect men get."

"Robbing the payroll and killing those soldiers is supposed to earn you respect?" Fargo said dubiously.

"The money will. Once we've set ourselves up in our new lives, with new identities."

In a way, Fargo did understand. Ruby had been right about there not being many jobs for women, and those there were paid less. Women weren't even allowed to vote. Some women back east had started to raise a fuss about it but so far not much had been done. "You say you like to do things smart but this strikes me as being dumb as hell."

"By robbing that payroll we've proved that women can do anything men can do," Big Bertha said.

"You couldn't have thought of a better way?"

"None that would give me a new start in life with enough money to do whatever I want."

"So the money does matter."

"I won't deny it helps."

Fargo scoured their vicinity. So far there was no sign of the Apaches. He hoped their luck held.

"Speaking of the money," Big Bertha said. "How about if we strike a deal of our own?"

"This should be interesting."

"I'll give you a thousand dollars out of my share if you'll ride off and forget about us. Tell the army you lost our trail. Or the Apaches got us. Anything you want."

"No."

"You can't use a thousand dollars? It'll buy a lot of drinks, a lot of ladies. Gamble to your heart's content."

"And Geraldine?"

Big Bertha brightened, thinking he would accept. "We'll dispose of her and no one will be the wiser."

"Except me."

"A thousand dollars will soothe your conscience right quick."

"I forget about the soldiers you killed. I forget about you sending Ruby to bushwhack me. I forget you tried to stomp me into the dirt. I forget everything and let you go your merry way."

"A thousand dollars," Bertha said again.

"I'll pass," Fargo said.

Bertha shook her head as if she couldn't believe what she was hearing. "Give me one good reason. You're not one of those sticklers for always doing right, are you?"

"Not hardly," Fargo said.

"Then why, damn it?"

Fargo looked her in the eyes. "I don't like you."

Bertha snorted, then cocked her head and said, "You're serious? You're taking all this personal?"

Fargo was going to tell her that he took everything personal but he decided not to waste his breath. A glance up the mountain showed Claire still climbing. It would be minutes yet before she reached the cliffs.

"You haven't answered me."

"I'm done flapping my gums." Fargo sat back and was placing the Henry in his lap when the Ovaro nickered.

The stallion was staring at a patch of brush about fifty feet away.

Shifting and raising the Henry, Fargo studied the brush and the ground around it.

"What's going on?" Big Bertha asked. "What has your horse bothered?"

"Quiet." Fargo concentrated on the brush. Something wasn't quite right. The middle part was darker than it should be. As if someone was crouched behind it.

"Is it the Apaches?" Bertha said. "Give me a gun so I can defend myself."

"Quiet, I said." Rising into a crouch, Fargo took a couple of steps.

"I insist," Bertha refused to shut up.

Fargo was about convinced it was nothing when he spied two brown dots, low down. *They were eyes.* The instant he saw them, they moved. An Apache half rose, spun, and ran.

Before Fargo could shoot, the warrior went to ground again.

"Go after him!" Big Bertha urged. "What are you waiting for?"

"You'd like that, wouldn't you?" Fargo said. She would grab her guns, or ride off, or both.

"Haven't you heard that the only good redskin is a dead one?"

Fargo didn't hate Indians just because they weren't white. And he didn't shoot them unless they were trying to do him in.

"What kind of scout are you?" Big Bertha scoffed.

Fargo didn't say anything. What would be the use?

"A scout who's an Injun lover," Bertha said in contempt. "Now I've heard everything."

For two bits, Fargo reflected, he'd shoot *her.*

"Folks say you're so tough. But you go easy on Apaches like you do on women," Big Bertha said. She placed her hands on the ground in front of her and bent toward him. "Nothing to say? Cat got your tongue?"

Fargo was watching for the Apaches.

"Yes, sir," Big Bertha babbled on. "You're nothing but a weak sister. You should give up scouting and be a store clerk. You won't have to hurt anybody at all."

Annoyed, Fargo turned. "You talk too much." He wondered if she was doing it on purpose. Maybe to distract him.

"I think this has gone on long enough," Big Bertha said.

"What has?"

"I tried to goad you into going after him so this would be over but you wouldn't. Very well. I'm nothing if not adaptable." Big

Bertha sighed. "I wanted to keep my little secret but we're wasting valuable time."

"Which secret would that be?"

"You'll appreciate it, I'm sure," Bertha said smugly. "You see, when I planned this out, I knew the worst danger we'd face wasn't from the boys in blue. It was from the Apaches."

"You got that part right, at least."

"If you'd gone after that one just now, they'd have jumped you."

"Another reason I didn't," Fargo said.

"Ah. But I'm tired of being held at gunpoint. It's time to end this so my girls and me can be on our way." Big Bertha smiled and raised her voice. "You might as well show yourselves, Grey Wolf."

And just like that, two Apaches seemed to rise out of the very earth with their rifles trained on Fargo, while the third rose over near the brush, his own rifle to his shoulder.

"Say hello to my friends," Big Bertha said.

28

Fargo had been watching for them yet they had snuck in practically under his very nose. To make a fight of it would be suicide. He might get one, maybe two, but not all three before they brought him down.

Big Bertha's broad face split in a gleeful grin. "Drop that Henry or die where you stand."

Fargo let go.

"Keep him covered," Big Bertha said. Rising, she stepped to her revolver and rifle and reclaimed them. Then, her eyes glittering with spite, she walked up to Fargo, chuckled, and rammed her rifle's stock into his belly.

Clutching his gut, Fargo fell to his knees. The pain wasn't as bad as he was letting on but he wanted them to think it was.

"That's for being such a nuisance," Big Bertha said.

The Apache by the brush came over. All three were as impassive as slabs of rock.

"Surprised?" Bertha gloated.

"These Apaches are with you?" Fargo said.

"Not with me, exactly." Bertha gestured at the tallest. "Grey Wolf, there, and his friends like their firewater. They buy it from a friend of mine who runs a saloon and sells whiskey to the Indians on the side. I asked him to put me in touch with them."

Fargo had to keep her talking until he was ready. "They helped you kill those soldiers?"

"No. I hired them for safe passage through Apache territory. A case of liquor for each of them for escorting us."

Fargo was stunned. The Apaches hadn't been shadowing the women with the intent of harming them. The warriors were protecting them, seeing to it that other Apaches left them alone. "Was it you who sent that one to kill me?"

"I asked Grey Wolf to take care of you, yes," Big Bertha said.

The tall warrior frowned. "Our friend not come back. Now we make you suffer, eh, white-eye?"

Fargo saw no point in telling them that it was Slits Throats who had slain the other warrior.

"Shoot him and get it over with," Big Bertha said.

"He kill Shis-Inday," Grey Wolf said. "We take him, kill him our way."

"How long will that take?" Bertha asked.

"He be a long time dying."

"What about me and my girls while you're having your fun?" Bertha said. "Who will protect us if other Apaches come along? You promised, damn you, and I'm holding you to your word."

Grey Wolf's craggy features hardened.

"If you want that whiskey, I damn well have a say," Big Bertha insisted. "The safety of me and my girls comes before anything. You hear me?"

The other two warriors hadn't said a thing. They were watching Grey Wolf and Bertha, caught up in the argument.

Fargo slowly lowered his arm. No one was paying attention to him. Their mistake. Bertha had made him drop the Henry but she'd forgotten about his Colt.

"We take him," Grey Wolf was saying. "We stake him out. We skin him. Cut out his eyes. Cut off his nose. He will die in two sleeps, maybe three."

"Two to three days? No, I say," Big Bertha said. "The army is after us. We can't hang around that long."

"Women not tell warriors what to do."

Big Bertha reacted as if he'd slapped her. "You damned redskin. You're no different than a white man. Looking down your nose at us because we're female. I have half a mind to shoot you."

Grey Wolf swung his rifle toward her. "You not threaten Apache."

One of the others turned his own rifle on Bertha.

Fargo couldn't have asked for anything better. The third warrior was still pointing a Spencer at him but watching Grey Wolf and Bertha.

"Damn you mangy redskins," she was saying. "I trusted you to keep your word and this is how you repay me?"

The moment had come. His hand a blur, Fargo drew and fanned a shot into the third warrior's chest. Without waiting to see the effect, he fanned a second shot into Grey Wolf, swiveled, and shot the other Apache in the face as the warrior jerked his rifle to his shoulder.

Grey Wolf staggered but didn't fall. His trigger finger tightened and the slug plowed into the earth next to Fargo's leg.

Fargo shot him in the forehead. All three were down, and he began to push to his feet.

Big Bertha had been rooted in shock but now she bellowed in rage and brought her own rifle to bear. "Die, you son of a bitch!" she screamed.

"Ladies first," Fargo said, and shot her in the chest. She was jarred but fired, and missed. Extending his arm, Fargo shot her in the cheek. That should have done it but she steadied herself and took aim. He fanned two swift shots at where her heart should be.

Big Bertha swayed. Her arms drooped and she sank down as if she were taking a seat, plopping hard on her bottom. Her eyelids fluttered, and she tried to say something.

"Just die," Fargo said.

Bertha let out a long breath and folded in on herself. The thud of her body hitting the ground was followed by the clatter of her rifle. Her legs twitched a few times and she was still.

Reloading the Colt, Fargo stood. He went to each of the Apaches, ensuring they were dead. When he looked up, someone was standing next to the manzanita. "I wondered where you got to."

Slits Throats came into the open. "I come to help you but you no need help."

127

"I was lucky," Fargo said.

Slits Throats nudged Bertha with his toe. "She was tough woman. Like buffalo cow."

Fargo suddenly remembered Geraldine and the others.

Up at the cliffs, the lady outlaws had reappeared. All four, along with their packhorses. They had heard the shots. Another flash of light made Fargo think one of them had unlimbered a rifle but they were too far off to hit him. There were more flashes, moving from rider to rider, which puzzled him.

On a hunch, Fargo went to Bertha's mount and rummaged in her saddlebags. He didn't find what he was looking for.

Fargo faced the cliffs. Those flashes were the spyglass. The women were passing it back and forth. They knew Big Bertha was dead. Or did they? They'd see her lying there, but they wouldn't be able to tell if she were breathing.

Quickly, Fargo moved to the body. Stooping, he sat Bertha up. It took some doing, as heavy as she was. Keeping himself between her and the others to block their view, he propped her against the manzanita.

Stepping back, Fargo mopped his brow. Hopefully, the women would think she was wounded and come down, bringing Geraldine Waxler with them. He stepped into the open and caught another flash. Raising an arm, he waved and beckoned.

The women didn't move.

"Take the bait," Fargo said out loud. He beckoned again, and could have whooped when they did. Three of them, anyway. The fourth, with the pack animals, stayed put.

Fargo frowned. There was no sign of Geraldine. He turned to ask Slits Throats if he'd caught sight of her, only to find the warrior had pulled his vanishing act again.

About twenty yards from the manzanita was a waist-high boulder. Fargo went over and stood behind it, the Henry cradled. He had a long wait but eventually the women drew near enough for him to tell which three it was: Claire, Theresa, and Alvena. Slowing, they spread out. Claire was in the middle, Theresa and Alvena to either side.

Claire drew rein well out from the boulder and the others followed her example. Rising in the stirrups, she looked toward the manzanita. "Bertha? Can you hear me?"

"She's been shot," Fargo said.

"Is she alive?"

"She needs doctoring," Fargo said.

Theresa raised her reins but Claire snapped a quick, "Stay put until we know what's what. I don't trust him."

"But Bertha . . ." Theresa began.

"Use your head," Claire said. "Do as Bertha taught us." She focused on Fargo. "What caused all the shooting?"

"The three Apaches," Fargo said.

Alvena was suspicious, too. "Why would they shoot? They're working with us, keeping us safe."

Fargo shrugged. "I don't know what it was about."

"He's lying," Alvena said to the others.

Claire cupped a hand to her mouth. "Bertha? If you're alive, answer us. Or move your arms. Something."

"She's unconscious," Fargo said, slowly sliding his right hand down the Henry to the hammer and the trigger.

"Bertha?" Claire tried one more time anyway.

A flash of light up at the cliffs told Fargo that Ruby was watching through the spyglass. "Is Geraldine Waxler still alive?" he asked.

"Forget her," Theresa said. "We're only interested in Bertha."

"Come see for yourself," Fargo said.

Theresa started to dismount but again Claire stopped her.

"No. He might be trying to trick us."

"We need to know," Theresa said. "She could be bleeding to death and we're just sitting here."

"I say we shoot him and then see how she is," Alvena said, and began to raise her rifle.

"No! If there's any chance at all Bertha is still alive, we owe it to her to keep her that way," Theresa argued.

Fargo waited. It would help if they came closer so he could drop all three. As extra incentive he said, "She's hurt bad. I don't have bandages but maybe you do."

"I'm going to her," Theresa declared, and swung down.

"No, damn it," Claire said.

"After all she's done for us," Theresa said, "you'd let her die without lifting a finger?"

"Bertha is already dead," Alvena said flatly. "She hasn't so much as twitched since we got here."

"I have to see for myself," Theresa said, and came toward the manzanita. "As for you," she said to Fargo, suddenly pointing her rifle at him, "if this is a trick, you'll regret it."

Claire raised her own rifle. "Be ready to protect her," she said to Alvena.

"Count on it," Alvena said.

Fargo thought of the slaughtered major and his men. He had meant it when he told Bertha he was through holding back. Time to do or die.

29

The woman called Theresa had her rifle pointed at Fargo, but in her worry for Big Bertha, she was staring at the body slumped against the manzanita.

Claire kept glancing between Fargo and Theresa and the tree.

Not Alvena. Her cheek was to her rifle and she didn't take her eyes off Fargo.

Fargo put on the poker face that had won him more pots than he could count. "Once you see she's alive, you can have her if you hand over Waxler."

Theresa and Claire both looked at their leader.

Fargo dropped behind the boulder. Alvena's rifle boomed, and he felt a sting in his cheek. Diving to one side, he fired as he struck the ground, but Alvena was already swinging low over her saddle, and he didn't think he'd hit her.

"Theresa! Look out!" Claire cried, and jerked her Henry to her shoulder.

Fargo shot her.

Shock rooted Theresa but only for a few seconds. Working her rifle's lever as she ran, she darted toward some mesquite.

Fargo shot her. He went for a chest shot but as he squeezed the trigger she twisted. He thought he caught her in the side.

Scrambling to his knees, Fargo hugged the boulder. It hadn't gone as he'd hoped. Now he was pinned down, and two, maybe three were still alive—Theresa in the mesquite, Claire somewhere by her mount, while Alvena had reined into a gully and wash and disappeared.

Silence fell.

Fargo inched his head around for a look-see and nearly lost an eye to a ricochet. The shot came from over where he'd last seen Alvena.

Splashes of red on Claire's saddle told him that she was hard hit. Since it wouldn't hurt to try, he hollered, "It doesn't have to be like this. Give yourselves up and I'll take you back to Fort Bowie."

"Go to hell!" Alvena yelled.

Over in the mesquite Theresa anxiously bawled, "Bertha? Bertha? Can you hear me?"

"Get it through your thick head she's dead," Alvena shouted. "The bastard tricked us."

Fargo was glad they were concentrating on him. It might have occurred to one of them to shoot the Ovaro to keep him from escaping if it came to that.

He saw Alvena's head pop up and banged off a quick shot that kicked dirt in her face.

Another boom, from the mesquite, chipped slivers from the boulder.

Claire hadn't joined in, which must have been why Theresa called out, "Claire? Are you still with us?"

There was no reply at first, and Fargo thought he must have got her. But no.

"I'm still here," Claire said, sounding as if she were in pain. "Don't worry about me."

More quiet, save for the buzz of a fly that took an interest in the nick in Fargo's cheek. Fargo swatted at it and must have exposed his arm because Alvena's rifle cracked and more slivers went flying. The woman was a good shot.

Fargo could use a swig from his canteen. His throat was dry, and he was sweating buckets.

"You couldn't let us get away, could you?" Theresa unexpectedly yelled. "You had to keep after us."

"Theresa, hush," Claire said.

"You're hurt, I can tell," Theresa responded, and raised her voice. "Fargo? What if I give you my entire share of the payroll to let us go? How would that be?"

Fargo saw no harm in answering. "Save your breath."

"Six thousand dollars," Theresa said. "That's more than most people make in ten years. All yours."

"What do I tell the army?" Fargo said. "That I lost a trail any ten-year-old could follow?"

"You don't have to tell them anything. Take the money and disappear. Go to Mexico. Or Canada. Hell, I don't care. You decide."

"I already did," Fargo said. "I take you back alive or I take you back dead. It's up to you."

"Fine," Theresa said bitterly. "Be that way."

More silence ensued. Fargo leaned his shoulder against the boulder and pulled his hat lower to keep the sun out of his eyes. He figured that the longer the standoff lasted, the better it was for him. The women must be as uncomfortable as he was, maybe more so. And Theresa and Alvena had to be worried about Claire. That might make them do something rash. But no sooner did he get his hopes up than they were dashed.

"Theresa? Alvena?" Claire hollered.

"I hear you," Theresa said.

"What?" from over at the gully.

"The two of you sneak away while I keep him here."

Fargo sat up.

"Forget that," Theresa said. "We're not leaving you. We lost Bertha. We won't lose you, too."

"Damn right, we won't," Alvena said.

"Listen to me," Claire said. "I'm done for. I don't know how much time I have left but it should be enough that I can keep him from going after you until you've gotten clean away."

"No," Theresa said.

"Absolutely not," Alvena echoed.

"Damn it," Claire said, her voice breaking with emotion. "Don't be so noble. I tell you I'm finished. I've lost too much blood. Get out of here and join Ruby and ride like hell. You have to get away. It's not right that Bertha died in vain."

"Hell, girl," Alvena said.

"You know I'm right."

"I don't like deserting you," Theresa said.

"You don't have to like it," Claire said. "Just do it before I'm too weak to lift my rifle."

"I hate this," Theresa declared.

No more was said. Fargo tried to spot Claire but couldn't. After about five minutes hooves clattered and Alvena broke into view, riding like a madwoman. He took aim but had to whip back when Claire fired, clipping the boulder.

When next Fargo looked, Alvena was out of range and had drawn rein. He thought she had changed her mind, but no. It wasn't long before Theresa appeared. Alvena swung her up behind her, and riding double, they continued on up the mountain.

"Now it's just you and me," Claire said, sounding happy that her friends were safe.

Fargo pegged her position as slightly to his left and not more than fifty feet away. Easing flat, keeping the boulder between them, he started to slide backward.

"Fargo?" Claire yelled. "I'd like to ask you something."

Fargo stopped.

"Are you there?"

"Where else would I be?" Fargo replied.

"Good. I have a question." Claire sounded weak. "Do you have a shred of sympathy in your soul?"

"*That's* what you want to ask?"

"I want you to put yourself in our shoes. Imagine what it's been like, having to lick men's boots all our lives. There are a lot of women who feel the same way."

Fargo considered that a poor excuse for shooting soldiers but he held his tongue.

"Are you still there?"

"Why do you keep asking that?" Fargo replied.

"You weren't saying anything. And I want to make you understand. To sympathize with us."

"Lady, some of those troopers you massacred had wives and families. Ask them if they feel sorry for you."

"What would it take to get you to let the others go?"

"Not a chance in hell," Fargo said.

"Please. I'm begging you."

Fargo had said all he was going to. He continued to slide back from the boulder, careful not to scrape the Henry or make some other noise that might give him away.

Claire cleared her throat. "I never wanted to spread my legs for money. I was forced into it by circumstance. I can't sew worth a lick, and I'm not much of a cook, so what else is there?"

Fargo put his hand on a flat rock and winced. It was hot enough to fry an egg.

"Are you listening? Are you still there?"

She was stalling, Fargo realized, trying to keep him talking to delay him from going after the others.

"Fargo?"

Moving faster, Fargo came to a wash. It was shallow but it would do. Snaking down into it, he commenced his stalk.

"Fargo? Don't ignore me. Please. You talked about families. Think of what it will mean to Alvena and Ruby and Theresa to have families of their own. The money lets them bury their pasts and start over."

Screened by mesquite, Fargo rose high enough to glance up the mountain.

Alvena and Theresa were almost to the cliffs.

"Granted, what we did was wrong," Claire prattled on. "But we were desperate. When Bertha came up with her brainstorm, we leaped at the chance. Can you blame us?"

Fargo wasn't about to answer.

"You can't imagine how much this means to us. Or the lengths we'll go to in order to carry it off."

Fargo raised his head higher, seeking a glimpse of her.

"Try to forgive us if you can. Try to remember we're only human. Try to . . ."

Fargo parted a patch of tall grass and there Claire was, on her belly facing the boulder. She heard the grass rustle and twisted around, bringing her rifle to bear. He had no chance to disarm her. No chance for anything but what he did—he shot her between her breasts.

"Oh!" Claire exclaimed, and dropped her Henry. Grimacing, she put her hand to a rapidly spreading scarlet stain.

Fargo went over. She still had her revolver, which he snatched from her holster and tossed. "I wish you'd given up when I told you to."

"So you do feel something?" Claire coughed and drops of blood formed at both corners of her mouth.

Fargo took it for granted she was on the verge of dying, and turned toward the Ovaro.

Suddenly lunging, Claire grabbed him around the ankle. "You're not going anywhere. I won't let you."

Fargo tried to tug free but she clung on. "What good does this do you?"

Looking up, Claire coughed and weakly smiled. "You can't blame a girl for trying."

"You are a tough bunch of ladies," Fargo said.

"We are, aren't we?" Claire's arms grew slack, and she let out a long breath and was gone.

"I hate this," Fargo said.

30

The cliffs were a vermilion color, the glare of the sun highlighting the red so that they appeared to be oozing blood.

Fitting, Fargo thought, as he climbed the last switchback, his hand on his Colt. He saw no trace of the women or their pack animals but their tracks were plain enough. The trail led him north along the base of the ramparts.

He had his hand on his Colt but saw no trace of the women.

Fargo was anxious to catch up before the outlaws harmed Geraldine. That they hadn't already puzzled him; they'd shown no compunctions about killing. But he hadn't come across her body.

He had gone a half mile when he was annoyed to see someone waiting for him up ahead. "You," he said as he drew near. "How did you get here before me?"

"I fly like bird," Slits Throats said.

Drawing rein, Fargo kept his hand on his Colt. "You're not mad about those other Apaches?"

"I not know them."

"So they're nothing to you?"

"They do what they want," Slits Throats said. "I do what I want. You savvy, white-eye?"

"I don't much savvy a damn thing about you," Fargo said, "or what sort of game you're playing."

"Game?"

"All the times you've vanished into thin air. Not helping me when I could have used some."

Slits Throats pointed at the cliff he was beside. "Help you now."

Fargo gigged the Ovaro to have a look. A dark patch he'd mistaken for a shadow was a gap wide enough for a horse. "Does this go through to the other side?"

"It does," Slits Throats said.

"I didn't know it was here," Fargo admitted. And a pass like this would usually be common knowledge.

"Few who not Apache do," Slits Throats said.

"The Apaches Big Bertha hired to protect them must have told the women about it."

Slits Throats grunted.

Fargo entered the gap. The walls practically brushed his stirrups, and when he craned his neck, he could barely see the top. It gave him a hemmed-in feeling he didn't like. He hoped the gap would go straight through but it curved every which way.

After him came Slits Throats, looking no more perturbed than if he were out for a Sunday ride.

"I'm obliged for you showing me," Fargo said.

"You find it soon anyway."

"I noticed you didn't help me down below when those women were trying to plant me."

"You need help to fight women, you not much man."

"It's good to know you care," Fargo said dryly.

"I care about hundred dollars and horse."

Fargo shifted in the saddle. "You wanted the money for a Henry, as I recollect."

Slits Throats nodded.

"Then we can part company. I left Claire's horse down there. It's yours if you want, and her rifle, besides." Fargo reckoned that would be that but he reckoned wrong.

"You promise me hundred dollars."

"To buy a repeater."

"I not want woman's rifle. I want buy my own."

"What difference does it make?" Fargo rejoined. One Henry was as good as another.

"Rifle not cost hundred dollars," Slits Throats said. "I have money left after I buy, yes?"

"You will," Fargo said.

"Then I want money."

Fargo scratched his chin in perplexity. "Why not take her horse and her rifle and be done with it? I'll give you forty dollars out of my own pocket. That's more than fair."

"I want hundred," Slits Throats insisted.

Fargo dropped the subject. It made no sense that he could see. But Slits Throats had proven helpful so he'd humor him.

More bends and turns brought them to a shelf that overlooked a desolate valley cut off from the outside world by cliffs higher than those they had passed through. "Where can these gals be heading?"

"We find out soon, eh."

Uncapping his canteen, Fargo took a swallow and offered it to Slits Throats.

"Not need any. I Apache. I not weak like white-eyes."

"You're only half Apache," Fargo said.

"It half that count."

A series of mostly open slopes brought them to the valley floor. They were easy targets but they reached the bottom without being shot at.

A maze of giant boulders in all shapes and sizes confronted them, ideal spots for an ambush. Drawing his Colt, Fargo rode with it resting on his leg. The heat was stifling, the stillness unnerving.

The clop of their mounts' hooves seemed unnaturally loud.

Fargo must have gone a quarter of a mile when it dawned on him that the only hoof falls he was hearing were the Ovaro's. He looked over his shoulder, and swore.

Once again, Slits Throats had disappeared.

Fargo wished he knew what the warrior was up to but for the time being he put the breed from his mind. He skirted a high slab of rock, a perfect rectangle with one end imbedded in the earth. Another massive formation reminded him of a bird's head. Yet another looked for all the world like a bear.

Patches of shade were welcome but did little to relieve the heat.

Fargo went around a mound of rock that must weigh tons and was about to mop his brow when he drew sharp rein.

Ahead was a clear space. Staked out in the center, her arms and legs spread-eagle, was Geraldine Waxler. She had also been stripped naked. Her eyes were closed, and there was a gash on her temple. Bruises marked her face and she had welts and black-and-blue marks on her arms and legs. Someone had whaled the tar out of her.

Quickly, Fargo reined around the rock. Dismounting, he shoved the Colt in his holster and shucked the Henry.

Whoever staked Geraldine out was using her as bait. They wanted him to rush in to help her, and be shot to pieces.

Sidling to where he could study the clearing and the terrain beyond, Fargo was careful not to show himself.

Across the way lay a jumble of boulders over half an acre in extent. He'd bet good money that someone was in there, waiting for him.

Fargo hunkered. Patience was called for. If they hadn't seen him, they might give themselves away.

Long minutes went by, the hot wind like the breath of a furnace.

Then Geraldine Waxler groaned. Her arms twitched, her eyelids fluttered, and she gave a start. She tried to rise, looked down at herself, and gasped. Licking her lips, she hollered, "Where are you? Why did you do this to me? I was doing everything you asked."

No one answered.

Geraldine struggled. Picket pins had been used to stake her out, pounded until they were nearly all the way in. Try as she might, she couldn't loosen them. After several attempts she subsided with a soft sob. "I know you can hear me. And I can guess why you did this."

Once again, no one replied.

"Fargo won't fall for it. He's not stupid, you know. You'll end up like your precious Bertha."

From the jumble of boulders came a snarl of anger. "Don't you dare insult her or I'll shoot you now and be done with you."

Fargo recognized the voice: Alvena's.

"Go to hell," Geraldine said. "What do I have to lose? Shoot me and I'm no use to you. He won't try to rescue me if I'm dead."

"He might not notice until it's too late," Alvena said. "Now shut your mouth or I'll come out there and beat on you some more."

Geraldine fell silent.

Fargo risked poking his head out farther in the hope she would see him but she had closed her eyes. He drew back before Alvena spotted him.

"Water," Geraldine croaked. "I need water."

"I told you to shut up," Alvena said.

"My throat is raw. I can't hardly breathe," Geraldine complained. "Give me some water, damn you."

"I'll give you something."

A shadow moved amid the boulders.

Alvena marched over to Geraldine and glared. "You don't have the sense God gave a goat, do you?"

"Where's your canteen?"

"Stupider than anyone," Alvena said, and without warning, she rammed her rifle's muzzle into Geraldine's belly.

Crying out, Geraldine thrashed wildly.

About to spring into the open, Fargo stopped cold.

Alvena had pointed her Henry at Geraldine's face and thumbed back the hammer. "Did that get your attention?"

"Damn you, damn you, damn you," Geraldine cried, her face contorted in pain.

"When I tell you to shut up, you'd better listen. The next time you make me come out here, I'll bust your teeth."

Geraldine didn't know when to leave well enough alone. "I hope he kills you like he did that cow you were so fond of."

Fargo had to hand it to her. The woman had grit.

Alvena was livid. Trembling with fury, she gouged the Henry into Geraldine's cheek. "You know what? I don't need you alive, after all. He's bound to come check whether you are or you aren't."

Uncowed, Geraldine shrieked, "Do it! I dare you! You miserable little bitch. If I wasn't tied down, I'd thrash you."

Alvena took a step back and aimed.

Taking a half step into the open to have a clear shot, Fargo raised his rifle. He fixed a bead—and had no one to shoot. Alvena had spotted him. Whirling, she sprinted for the jumbled boulders, firing as she went. He was forced to duck or take lead.

"Skye? Is that you?" Geraldine shouted.

Fargo took another look. Alvena was in the boulders, somewhere. He drew back just as her rifle spanged.

"Skye?" Geraldine anxiously cried. "Did she get you?"

Fargo intended to let Alvena wonder if she had or she hadn't. Let it fray at her nerves a while.

Until Alvena yelled, "How about it, *Skye*? Answer the lady. If you don't, I'll start putting holes in her. Her knees, then her elbows, maybe shoot off her nose while I'm at it."

Fargo smacked the rock in frustration.

"You don't have all day," Alvena said. "I'll count to three and commence."

31

"One!"

Fargo didn't charge into the open and get shot down, as Alvena wanted. He ran to his left, avoiding the open space.

"Two!"

Fargo poured on speed.

"Say good-bye to—" Alvena shouted, and stopped.

Ducking, Fargo weaved. She'd spotted him. Her first shot sizzled past his head. Her next struck a boulder. He was a third of the way around but it wasn't nearly enough. He flung himself behind another boulder a heartbeat before her third shot screamed off the top.

"You son of a bitch!" Alvena railed. "You're like a damn rabbit. But if I can't hit you, I can sure as hell hit her."

"No!" Geraldine cried.

Fargo looked out just as Alvena fired.

A crimson geyser erupted from Geraldine's leg. Shrieking, she bucked against the ropes.

A puff of gun smoke gave Fargo some idea where Alvena was. He fired to keep her pinned down, worked the lever, fired again.

Heaving up, Fargo tried to close the gap. Geraldine was writhing and sobbing but there was nothing he could do. He thought he saw a rifle muzzle poke out of the boulders and fired at it. He was wrong. Another puff of gun smoke at a different spot caused him to dive flat.

Alvena cackled. She was enjoying herself.

Frantic by now, Geraldine was doing all in her power to free herself. In her frenzy she loosened the pin holding her left arm but couldn't pull the pin all the way out.

Alvena's rifle cracked.

Geraldine's left elbow ruptured, and she let out the loudest shriek yet. "No! No! No!"

Sheer rage seized Fargo. A red mist seemed to fill his eyes, and he barreled at the boulders.

Alvena's next shot blew Geraldine's right elbow to ruin. Geraldine opened her mouth wide but the only sounds that came out were inarticulate whines. The whites of her eyes were showing.

Fargo was almost to the jumble and still didn't see Alvena. Emptying the Henry, he dropped behind a slab.

"Nice try," Alvena mocked him. "But not good enough."

A rifle barrel appeared.

Setting the Henry down, Fargo drew his Colt, and went to rush in.

A part of Geraldine's face showered around her in bits and pieces.

"No!" he roared. Beside himself, he plunged into an opening, and there Alvena was, turning toward him and jacking her rifle lever.

Fargo fanned his Colt.

The slug canted Alvena onto the tips of her toes but she gamely brought her rifle up.

Fargo fired again, and once more.

Alvena twisted to the impacts. She pressed her rifle to her shoulder but she was wobbling.

He shot her in the head.

The thud of her body brought him out of himself. The red mist slowly faded, as did his rage. He swallowed, and walked over.

In death Alvena's features mirrored the hate she'd shown in life. Her lips were split in a feral grimace.

Fargo raised a boot to stomp her but lowered it again. "No," he said out loud. He wouldn't stoop to her level. Quickly, he went back out, reloading at he went. He scooped up the Henry along the way.

Geraldine was trembling and making ugly wet gurgling sounds. With good reason. Her mouth had been blown away, leaving a cavity that bubbled with blood. It flowed over what was left of her chin and down her neck, spreading in a puddle. Her eyes were haunted pools of terror.

Sinking to a knee, Fargo squeezed her hand. He wanted to tell her he'd tried his best but the words wouldn't come.

Geraldine tried to speak. More bubbles formed in the blood in her mouth and made popping sounds as they burst.

Helpless, Fargo bowed his head. Her fingers stiffened in his, and then relaxed. When he looked up, it was over. "Thank God," he said. He closed her eyes, and stepped back.

Fargo hankered to climb on the Ovaro and go after the last two, to end it once and for all. But Geraldine deserved better than to be gorged on by vultures and other scavengers.

It took half an hour to find enough rocks to cover her. The ground was too hard for digging, and he didn't have anything to dig with even if it wasn't.

He piled the rocks high to smother the scent of the blood.

At last Fargo stepped back and regarded his handiwork. He looked at the sky, shook his head, and picked up the Henry. Reloading, he shoved it into the scabbard.

The sun was on its westward trek, the heat as blistering as ever.

As he rode, Fargo felt strangely numb. He'd seen a lot of people shot in his wanderings but this one got to him. He couldn't say why. Geraldine wasn't a friend, or even a lover. Maybe it was the brutality of it. Maybe that a woman was to blame. Although if there was one thing he'd learned, it was that females could be as deadly, and merciless, as any male.

Nightfall found him in chaparral country. He sought their campfire but they were too smart to give themselves away. Forcing himself to stop, he spread out his bedroll.

He lay staring at the stars but not seeing them.

In his mind's eye he saw Geraldine's mouth exploding, again and again and again. It wasn't like him to be so morbid, and with a growl of annoyance, he rolled onto his side.

The tank he knew about was now miles to the south. He imagined plunging his face in the cool water and drinking until he was fit to burst. But the outlaws weren't going anywhere near it. To go there would delay him half a day, a delay he couldn't afford.

He wasn't aware of falling asleep but the next he knew, dawn was breaking. He didn't bother with coffee, didn't have enough water left for a pot anyhow. He wet the Ovaro's muzzle and his own lips and was on his way while the sky was still gray.

It soon became apparent the women hadn't stopped for the night.

Good, Fargo thought. Their animals were tired. They'd have to halt before the morning was out to let them rest.

The prospect of having them in his gun sights brought a grim smile.

When Slits Throats came alongside, Fargo scowled. "Look who it is."

"You not sound happy to see me," the warrior said.

"About as happy as I'd be if I swallowed a cactus."

"What I do now?"

"Geraldine Waxler was shot to pieces yesterday. Once again, I could have used your help. Once again, you were off playing at being a ghost."

"You need think about something else," Slits Throats said. "What you do when you reach gold camp?"

"Gold camp?" Fargo said in surprise, and drew rein.

Slits Throats nodded and stopped. "Some whites find yellow rocks. It bring other whites come from all over."

A new strike lured the greedy in droves. Gold, silver, it didn't matter. They swarmed in like locusts in the hope of striking it rich.

"Now many whites," Slits Throats said. "Call place Gold Gulch."

"How long ago was this?"

"Three, maybe four moons."

Moons were months. No wonder Fargo hadn't heard of it. He hadn't been through this territory in a coon's age. "How far?"

Slits Throats pointed. "Over next range. Women probably already there."

Unless they went around, which Fargo considered unlikely. Their horses were worn out, and they must be in need of food and rest, themselves.

"I not go in Gold Gulch," Slits Throats let him know. "They not like Apaches. Or any Indians."

"I'm going in," Fargo said. "You'll get your money when I ride out."

"If you ride out."

Below a ridge dominated by a high peak stretched a serpentine gulch six to seven miles long. At some points it was only a couple of hundred feet across, at other spots, a quarter of a mile.

On the other side a tent city had sprouted. Scores in different sizes. A few shacks had been erected, the wood coming from a tract of woodland. A spring was in there somewhere.

Fargo started down. By the time he reached the gulch, Slits Throats was no longer behind him.

Ore hounds of every age and description had staked out sites and were digging and picking and sifting as if their lives depended on it. More than a few crudely painted signs had been posted warning others to stay off their claims.

The gulch walls were sheer rock for much of its length but here and there breaks allowed access.

Fargo wound down the first one he came to and at the bottom was confronted by one of the signs.

Almost immediately a scruffy specimen in dirty homespun and a straw hat barred his way and brandished a shotgun.

"What in hell do you reckon you're doin', mister?"

Fargo was patient with him. The man was only protecting his claim. "I'd like to cross to the other side."

"Where did you come from?" the man asked. "There's nothin' up yonder but wild country."

"From Fort Bowie."

"You crossed all that Apache country by your lonesome?" the prospector marveled.

"It wasn't easy," Fargo said.

"You must have heard about the strike. How men are pullin' ore out of the ground as big as your fist." The man frowned. "It ain't true."

"The gold is all yours, friend," Fargo said. "I'm on army business."

The man looked him up and down. "If you don't mind my sayin', you look like hell." He moved aside. "Go ahead if you want. I don't take you for a claim jumper."

"I'm obliged."

Suspicious stares were cast Fargo's way but no one else tried to stop him as he crossed the gulch to a trail that brought him to the tent city. Another sign announced this was GOLD GULCH. Below the name someone with a sense of humor had scrawled POPULATION and a question mark.

The tents had been put up wherever it struck their owner's fancy. The result was no semblance of order whatsoever. Entering was like entering a maze.

Fargo let his nose guide him. He had gone without whiskey for so long that the scent drew him like honey drew a bear. A particularly large tent had SALOON written on its sides and over the front flaps, which were tied open. Inside, ore hounds, gamblers, doves and more mingled in raucous pursuit of life's pleasures.

Fargo added the Ovaro to a long row of waiting animals, and

went in. He intended to ask if Gold Gulch had a stable. If not, he'd head over to the woods and see if he was right about a spring.

No sooner did he step past the flaps than a buxom blonde in a tight dress sashayed up and hooked her arm with his.

"What do we have here? I do believe I've struck the mother lode. How do you do, handsome? My name is Wendelin."

Her perfume reminded Fargo of lilacs. "How about I treat you to a drink and you answer a few questions?"

"I'm partial to Scotch," Wendelin informed him.

The bar consisted of planks supported by barrels. Two barkeeps were busy as bees.

Fargo paid for a Scotch for Wendelin and Monongahela for himself. They touched glasses, and sipped. Whiskey had seldom tasted so good.

"What was that about questions?" Wendelin said.

Fargo learned there was no stable but a man named Carver sold grain and water at a tent farther in. "I'm also looking for a pair of ladies."

"What's wrong with me?" Wendelin teased, and wiggled her hips. "I can do anything they'll do, and then some."

Fargo chuckled. He described Ruby and Theresa, adding, "They would have ridden in earlier."

"Sorry. I've been working all day, and they didn't come in here." Wendelin raised her glass, and blinked. "I'll be damned."

"What?"

Wendelin motioned at the entrance. "Isn't that one of them now?"

32

"I'll be damned," Fargo echoed her.

Ruby was out near the horses. She had her Henry and was gazing intently about.

Almost too late, Fargo realized what she was doing. Slipping between Wendelin and the bar, he slumped down.

"What on earth are you doin'?" Wendelin asked.

"Stand still," Fargo said. He had a hunch that Ruby had spotted the Ovaro and was hunting for him.

"You playin' some sort of hide-and-seek?" Wendelin asked in amusement.

Fargo peeked over at her.

Ruby had turned toward the Ovaro, and for a few moments Fargo feared she'd try to steal it. But no. Wheeling on a heel, she strode off.

Gulping the rest of the Monongahela, Fargo set the empty glass on the plank. "I'll be back, gorgeous," he said, and smacked Wendelin on her fanny.

She laughed merrily. "I hope so."

Fargo hurried out. He glimpsed Ruby going around a tent and ran to catch up. He almost collided with a man coming out of a tent and the man cussed and told him to watch where he was going.

He came to where he'd last seen Ruby. She wasn't anywhere in sight. Worse, she could have gone any of a number of ways.

Fargo sprinted straight ahead and after a minute realized it was the wrong direction. He veered right, running around tent after tent, but no Ruby. He tried to the left of where he'd seen her, with the same result.

He'd lost her.

Fargo reckoned the women must be holed up somewhere, but where? He asked a gent in a frock coat and wide-brimmed hat if Gold Gulch had a hotel and the man chuckled.

"Where do you think you are, mister? St. Louis?"

"There's nothing at all?"

"There are some tents where you can pay for a cot for the night," the gambler enlightened him.

"Do any of them take women?"

"You have to ask around. I have my own tent, so I wouldn't know."

Fargo returned to the saloon, and the Ovaro. Mounting, he rode in search of the man who sold grain and water. It took longer than he liked but it was worth it for the stallion's sake. He asked if the man had seen anything of two women in men's clothes and the man looked at him as if he were loco.

How to find them? Fargo wondered. It would take days to cover the entire camp from end to end. By then they'd be long gone.

Twilight was falling when Fargo made his way to the saloon yet again. He tied the Ovaro where he could keep an eye on it and went in.

Work had stopped in the gulch for the day, and many of the gold seekers were drifting into camp for a night's entertainment.

Fargo shouldered his way to the bar. He paid for a bottle and roved the tables until a chair emptied. Claiming it, he spent the next hour and a half playing poker. Lady Luck favored him. His twenty dollars became sixty. The next hand, he was dealt a full house. He went all in and won another sixty.

By then lanterns had been lit. The liquor flowed like water. Men who had toiled hard all day in the heat of the blazing sun for a few nuggets gambled them away at cards or faro or dice, or drank them away with the bug juice of their choice. Tomorrow they'd back in the gulch, breaking backs from dawn until dusk, and lose whatever they dug out all over again.

Fargo's cards had turned cold when a warm hand brushed the nape of his neck. Perfume wreathed him, and a friendly voice purred in his hear.

"The boss is letting me off in ten minutes or so," Wendelin said. "Any interest in walking a girl home?"

Fargo knew he shouldn't. He needed to find Ruby and Theresa. But an extra hour wouldn't hurt. "I'll be here."

The ten minutes were about up when someone poked his shoulder. He glanced up, thinking it was Wendelin.

"You're in my chair, mister."

The newcomer was rake thin, with a sallow complexion. He wore a bowler, a suit, and expensive boots. The gun belt around his waist was decorated with silver studs. His Remington had ivory grips.

Fargo took him for a gambler. "You can have it when I'm done," he said.

Smiling coldly, the man in the bowler took a couple of steps back. "You're done now."

"Go pester someone else."

A gray-haired man across the table bent toward him. "You shouldn't ought to talk to him like that. Don't you know who he is?"

"A nuisance," Fargo said.

"That's Leferty," the gray-haired player said.

"He's a gunhand," another threw in.

Leferty slid his hand close to his holster. "I won't say it again, mister. Get out of that chair."

Fargo set down his cards. "Are you drunk?" It was the only reason he could think of for the man to goad him into drawing.

"Sober as can be," Leferty said. "I never drink when I work."

"Work?" Fargo said, and insight hit him like a punch between the eyes. He was being provoked on purpose.

"When you're ready," Leferty said, "go for your six-shooter."

"You're that sure of yourself?"

"Take a good look at my pistol," Leferty said. "Count the notches for yourself."

Fargo did. There were nine. "Well, now," he said.

"You can stand up," Leferty said. "I like it to be fair."

"Damned decent of you." Fargo pushed back his chair. "How much are they paying you?"

"Who?"

"Don't be a jackass," Fargo said.

"Four hundred dollars."

The gray-haired player whistled, then said, "Mr. Leferty, sir, do you mind the rest of us get out of the way?"

"Do whatever you want, old-timer," the gunhand said.

Chairs scraped, and the card players retreated. It drew the attention of others, and whispers began to spread.

Fargo rose and faced the would-be assassin. "How do you fit in? Are you part of their gang?"

"What gang?" Leferty said. "They asked around, looking for a shooter, and someone recommended me. I'm pretty well-known hereabouts."

"You're about to be pretty dead." Fargo was curious. "Did they tell you who I am?"

"No, and I never ask. Names don't matter. Only the dying, and the money."

"Did they pay you in advance?"

"You ask a lot of questions."

Fargo asked another. "Where can I find them when it's over?"

"Now who is sure of himself?" Leferty said. Backing off another step, he turned sideways to make himself harder to it. "Start the dance whenever you're of a mind."

"Jackasses first," Fargo said.

"I gave you your chance," Leferty said, and his hand flicked.

Fargo had his Colt out before the assassin. He fired as Leferty cleared leather, fired as Leferty staggered, fired as Leferty's legs slowly buckled and he oozed to the ground.

"God in heaven," someone said.

A hush fell. No one moved. No one seemed to breathe.

Fargo reloaded, taking his time. He finished, twirled the Colt into his holster, and went to the body. No one objected when he helped himself to the killer's poke.

The gray-haired gent cleared his throat. "We all saw it, mister. It was self-defense. Not that it matters. Gold Gulch don't have any law."

Fargo stood. Since he had everyone's attention, he took advantage. "Two women," he said, and described Ruby and Theresa once more. "They hired this hombre to kill me. Anyone who tells me where to find them gets fifty dollars."

There were no takers.

Scooping up his winnings, Fargo placed them in the poke. Not a soul interfered as he backed out. The Ovaro was dozing but roused when he opened his saddlebags and slid the bottle in.

Out of the saloon hustled Wendelin. She was waving a bottle of her own, and called out, "Hold on there, handsome. Did you forget about me?"

Truth to tell, Fargo had. "No," he said.

"That's good to hear," Wendelin said in delight. "I was worried that jasper might have spoiled your mood."

Draping an arm around her, Fargo said, "Forget a pretty gal like you? How about you show me to this room of yours?" He snagged the Ovaro's reins.

"With pleasure."

Wendelin puffed herself up and strolled along as if she were a queen showing herself off. "That was some shootin' back there. I never saw anybody as fast as you. Folks will talk about it for days."

"Folks do love to flap their gums."

"Me, I'm partial to pokin' more than flappin'," Wendelin said.

Fargo could stand to relax for a spell, himself. A lot had happened since daybreak, and he had a feeling the worst was yet to come. "Makes two of us."

"Good," Wendelin said, and pecked him on the cheek. "We'll have us a grand time."

They weren't followed, as near as Fargo could tell. Her place turned out to be another tent. A bed filled a third of it. The only other furniture was a chair, and a lantern hung from the center brace.

"Cozy," Fargo said.

"Ain't it, though," Wendelin said, patting the bed. "I had it brought in from Tucson. Cost me a pretty penny for the freight but it's worth it. Most men like a bed better than a cot."

"I'm one of them," Fargo said. Cots were uncomfortable as hell. Sinking into the chair, he opened his bottle.

Wendelin plopped onto the bed and playfully kicked her legs high in the air, causing her dress to slip down around her thighs. "You plannin' to get drunk first?"

Fargo would love to but he needed his wits about him. Ruby and Theresa might take it into their heads to hire another killer. As much money as they had, they could hire a whole army.

"Are you?" Wendelin said when he didn't answer.

"Just enough to wet my whistle," Fargo said, chugging. He noticed that she hadn't tied the tent flaps, got up, and began to tie them himself.

"Afraid we'll be disturbed?"

"Not much privacy in a place like this." Fargo was thinking of more gunhands.

"Not in a tent, no." Wendelin snickered. "But don't you worry. It goes against my grain but I'll keep the ruckus down."

Done with the flaps, Fargo moved to the bed. "I should be honest with you."

"You're not into something strange, are you? Like that lunkhead who wanted his dog to watch. Or that time a miner wanted to do it in the dark in his mining duds."

"There are people out to kill me."

150

"No foolin'."

"They might try again."

Wendelin placed her foot on his leg and ran it up and down his thigh. "If I'm not worried, you shouldn't be. Hell, a little danger will add some spice."

"You could take a bullet."

"I'll be so busy gushing, I doubt I'd notice."

Now it was Fargo who laughed. "Just don't say I didn't warn you."

"The only thing I want to hold," Wendelin said, lightly rubbing her sole over his manhood, "is that pecker of yours."

"Let's get to it, then," Fargo said, and stretched out on the bed beside her.

"Your spurs. Bedspreads and sheets cost money."

"Yes, ma'am."

Wendelin bent and peeled off white net stockings, casting each aside with a toss of her foot. She had nicely firm legs, and when she parted them, gave him a glimpse of alabaster thighs. "Like what you see?"

Fargo grunted while undoing his gun belt and his pants.

"Men," Wendelin said. She started in on her buttons and stays and shed her dress with a speed borne of a lot of practice. Her chemise was next. Propping herself on an elbow, she cupped one of her breasts and wriggled it at him. "Still like what you see?"

Did Fargo ever. Her melons were large, her tummy flat, her waist narrow for her size. A golden triangle crowned her womanhood. Without realizing it, he licked his lips.

"Good Lord," Wendelin said in mock horror. "Are you fixin' to eat me?"

"There's an idea," Fargo said thickly. Swooping his mouth to a nipple, he inhaled it and swirled it with his tongue. She cooed softly and entwined her fingers in his hair, knocking his hat off in the process. Her other hand drifted lower and she uttered a tiny gasp.

"My, oh my. What have I found here?"

Fargo's hunger for her mounted. Pressing her onto her back, he kissed her face, her neck, her cleavage. For her part, Wendelin couldn't get enough of his pole. She rubbed and stroked and turned his blood to fire in his veins.

"I think the pump is primed," she said with a grin.

Fargo couldn't even grunt for the knot in his throat.

"Ready when you are, big man. And I do mean 'big.'"

33

Fargo was more than ready. His hands caressing her thighs, he knelt between them.

Gasps of pleasure fluttered from Wendelin's lips. Raising her hips, she rubbed against him, making him wet from tip to stem. Pushing her breasts into his chest, she bit his shoulder and dug her fingernails into his back.

Fargo squeezed one, hard.

"Yes, oh yes," Wendelin gasped. With a deft movement, she impaled herself on his pole, enveloping him in her velvet sheath. Wrapping her legs around his waist, she kissed him, panting into his mouth even as she pumped her hips.

Fargo matched her stroke for stroke. He could feel her triangle brush his skin, feel her contract inside, feel the wild beat of her heart under his fingers. Wendelin was one of those women who gave as passionately as she got. One of those women who genuinely liked to make love.

"Oh God, oh God, oh God."

Fargo was on the verge. Gritting his teeth, he held off.

His partner, on the other hand, was in the grip of carnal abandon. She moved ever faster, ever harder. Closing her eyes, she bit her lip, evidently to keep from crying out. And then she was there. She exploded violently, bucking and thrashing. It was a wonder her bed held together.

As for Fargo, he let himself go, savoring the violent throbs of pleasure she gave him. After a while they coasted to a stop, and he rolled off her onto his side, completely spent.

"You magnificent stallion, you," Wendelin breathed. "It's too bad we can't do that a few more times."

"Who says we can't?" Fargo said. A short rest, and he would take her again.

Wendelin didn't answer. Snuggling against him, she kissed his shoulder and his arm. "Damn," she said.

"What?"

Again she didn't reply.

Fargo didn't think much of it. He closed his eyes, resting. He felt her move and cracked them open again to see what she was doing. She had slid a hand under her pillow and was pulling the pillow toward her.

"I've had to do it before, you know," Wendelin said. "That time a drunk tried to beat me. And that fella who wanted a patch of my skin as a keepsake. But this is different. This is for my nest egg."

Wondering what she was talking about, Fargo saw her glance at his face.

"When you saw her, she wasn't looking for you. She was coming back to talk to me. I knew her in Tucson."

Fargo realized she meant Ruby.

"I knew Big Bertha, too."

Her hand swept from under her pillow and clutched a pearl-hilted dagger. Fargo barely threw himself back in time. The double-edged blade ripped into the bed, missing him by a hair. Seizing her wrists, he rolled and kicked and sent her tumbling to the floor. He was on his feet in a twinkling but so was she.

Naked, the dagger glittering, Wendelin stalked toward him. "I'm sorry. I truly am. But it's more money than I'd earn in a month of Sundays."

Backing away, Fargo desperately pulled at his pants. He couldn't do much with them down around his ankles. He got them to his thighs just as she lunged. Sidestepping, he retreated farther.

"Damn, you're quick."

Fargo's hands were free but his Colt was on the other side of the bed, and if he bent to get his toothpick, she'd plant that blade. Stalling, he said, "You're working with Ruby?"

"She and that other gal showed up about the middle of the morning," Wendelin said while moving her dagger back and forth. "First thing they did was stop at the saloon. You're not the only one who likes a drink. That's when I saw her and went over to get reacquainted."

"And she offered you money to kill me."

Wendelin nodded. "Said you were after them but didn't say why. Said you'd murdered Big Bertha. Said she'd pay me if I kept my eyes peeled and if you showed up, did her a favor."

"And here we are," Fargo said. He had been circling toward the chair and it was almost in reach.

153

"I thought I wore you out. I thought you'd be easy."

Fargo stopped. "Drop the blade and step back, and I'll leave, no hard feelings."

"Can't."

"Then this is on you."

Wendelin came at him fast and low. Whirling, Fargo gripped the chair and swung it with all his force, full at her knife arm and head. There was the crack of a bone breaking, and the chair itself shattered.

Crying out, Wendelin pitched to the ground, her dagger skittering under the bed. She tried to rise, and collapsed.

Fargo threw down what was left of the chair. Hunkering, he felt for a pulse. Her nose was broken, her ear was pulped, and she'd have to wear a sling for a month or more, but she'd live. He smothered an impulse to tend to her. She'd tried to kill him. She could go to hell and take Ruby and Theresa with her.

Mulling what she'd told him, Fargo dressed and strapped on his Colt. He had gone from being the hunter to the hunted. First Leferty, the gunhand, and now Wendelin. Who knew how many others Ruby and Theresa had sicced on him?

Reclaiming his bottle, Fargo jammed his hat on and loosened the tent ties. The Ovaro was dozing. No one was in sight so he slipped out, slid the Monongahela into his saddlebags, and mounted.

Gigging the stallion, Fargo went around another tent. Several men were coming toward him. He tensed but they walked on by, talking and joking and paying no attention to him.

By now, Fargo reasoned, Ruby and Theresa had heard about Leferty. Would they run? Theresa might, but not Ruby. Ruby would want to finish it.

With the advent of night, most of the tents glowed with lamp and lantern light. Tinny piano music filled the night, along with boisterous voices and merry laughs. Now and then an angry curse was heard. Once, a shot.

Fargo saw no sign of Ruby and her friend. They didn't have a tent of their own, so they might be camped at the outskirts of Gold Gulch. Unless they'd bought a tent, or paid someone else to use theirs.

Fargo was so deep in thought that when a man was silhouetted against a backdrop of glowing canvas, raising a rifle, he was a shade slow to react. The rifle boomed but the man rushed his aim. Drawing, Fargo fanned three swift shots of his own and had the satisfaction of seeing the figure crash against the tent and fall.

Reining away, Fargo got out of there before he was badgered with questions. Shouts broke out. When they faded, he stopped and reloaded. "So that's how it's going to be," he said grimly. Cat and mouse, with him the mouse.

From then on he stuck to the shadows, riding in ever wider loops until he reached the edge of the camp.

Here and there campfires dotted the plain. Dozens lit the gulch, itself. Not everyone had a tent, or wanted one. To check each fire would take the entire night, and he still might not find them.

Fargo had seldom been so frustrated. He turned back into Gold Gulch and headed for the saloon. Maybe, just maybe, Ruby would come back there.

By avoiding bright areas, Fargo reached the saloon without incident. The place was busier than ever. He stopped in a patch of shadow and sat watching for more than half an hour. He had about decided he was wasting his time when two women appeared from around the side.

It was Wendelin and Theresa, the latter with her arm around the former, helping her. Wendelin's arm was in a crude sling. Her nose was swollen to twice its normal size, and one of her eyes was discolored. They drew stares as they entered and made their way to a table where five men were playing cards.

One of the men got to his feet. Taller than most, he wore a buckskin shirt and store-bought pants. His hat had a high crown and the front rim was curled down. On his right hip was a revolver, on his left a bowie.

Wendelin apparently knew him. She put her arm on his shoulder, and he bent his face to hers, probably so he could hear over all the noise. Several times she motioned with her good arm at Theresa.

The tall man straightened, and nodded. He said something to two of the other card players and they rose and joined him. Both had the air of two-legged wolves.

With Theresa helping Wendelin, the five of them emerged from the saloon. The three men climbed on horses and followed the women around the side.

Careful to stay well back, Fargo followed. They weren't in any hurry, which made it easier. He thought they were making for

Wendelin's tent but they presently stopped at another. The men dismounted and all five went in.

Swinging down, Fargo shucked his Colt. On cat's feet he glided around to the rear of the tent and put his ear to the green canvas.

Wendelin was speaking. ". . . of the toughest hombres I know. Him and his pards can get the job done."

"That's what you said about Leferty."

Fargo tingled with elation. That was Ruby.

"Leferty made the mistake of bracing Fargo," Wendelin said. "Cullen, here, won't be that stupid."

"I sure as hell won't," Cullen said.

"You understand it has to be done quickly?" Ruby said. "For reasons I can't explain, we have to leave as soon as we can. But we don't want to show ourselves with him out there hunting through the entire camp."

"How much?" Cullen asked.

"A thousand dollars."

One of the hard cases gave a snort of surprise. "You must really want this scout dead, lady."

"You have no idea," Ruby said.

"Half now," Cullen said, "and half when he's dead."

"No," Ruby said.

An edge came into Cullen's voice. "What are you tryin' to pull? We're not killin' him for free."

"I paid Leferty and another man half in advance and look at how that turned out. They're both dead and I'm out that money." Ruby paused. "You want the thousand? You earn it. You kill him and I'll give you the full amount."

"How do we know we can trust you?" Cullen said.

"Wendelin will vouch for me," Ruby told him. "We've been friends a good many years."

"That we have," Wendelin said. "Take my word for it, Cullen. If she says she'll pay you, she will."

"She'd better," Cullen said. "She tries runnin' out on us, she'll regret it."

"No need for threats," Ruby said. "Besides, I don't have the money with me. It's with our horses, and they're well hid."

Fargo frowned.

"So will you or won't you?" Ruby was saying. "Because if you won't, I'm sure we can find others who will."

156

"We'll do it," Cullen said. "All you have to do is tell us where to find him."

"How would I know?" Ruby retorted. "I've been here all night."

"Don't look at me," Wendelin said. "I have no idea where he got to after he hit me with my chair."

"We can't search the whole damn camp," Cullen said. "That would take days."

"Find him," Ruby said. "There has to be a way."

"Hell," one of the other men said.

"Let's go," Cullen said. "We'll ask around. Could be someone has seen him."

"His horse is like a pinto," Ruby said. "If that helps."

"What the hell does that mean?" Cullen said. "Either it is or it ain't."

"I don't know how else to describe it," Ruby said. As an afterthought she added, "Oh. And it's a stallion. A big one."

"Come on," Cullen said, apparently to his pards.

"I'm going back to the saloon," Wendelin announced. "I need to let my boss know I won't be much use for a while."

Fargo heard the tent flap rustle. Their footsteps faded, and he started around the other side, thinking to catch Ruby and Theresa off guard. A sudden yell from a short distance away brought him to a stop. There was a commotion, and the tent opened again.

"Look at what we found!" Wendelin hollered.

Fargo crept to the front corner. One look, and he cursed himself for a fool.

The man called Cullen had hold of the Ovaro's reins and was leading it back, his pards on either side.

Wendelin, walking ahead of them, giggled and motioned. "It was over yonder, just standing there."

Framed in the opening, Ruby and Theresa looked at each other and Ruby put her hand on her six-shooter. "The hell you say."

"What's the matter?" Wendelin said. "You wanted him found, didn't you? His horse is a start."

"You damn simpleton," Ruby snapped. "Don't you get it? If his horse is here, he must be, too. Instead of us finding him, he's found us."

"Oh, hell," Wendelin said.

"He's probably watching us right this second," Ruby said.

"In that case," Cullen said, "there's only one thing to do." Drawing his revolver, he pointed it at the Ovaro's head. "Show yourself, mister!" he yelled. "Or they'll be feeding your horse to the dogs."

34

Fargo never hesitated. Lowering the Colt behind his leg, he stepped out where they could see him. "Looking for me?"

Even though they were expecting it, the suddenness of his appearance seemed to surprise them. Ruby and Theresa spun, and Theresa exclaimed, "It's him." Wendelin folded her good arm over her broken arm as if afraid he'd hit her again. The man called Cullen moved his revolver closer to the Ovaro while his two friends swooped their hands to their hardware.

"I wouldn't," Fargo said.

"You don't have a say," Cullen said. "Not if you want your horse to live."

Ruby, beaming, put her hands on her hips. "At last I have you where I want you. I can pay you back for Bertha, Claire and Alvena." She tilted her head. "Alvena is dead, isn't she? You wouldn't be here if she weren't."

"Dead as hell," Fargo said.

"I can't tell you how much I hate you," Ruby said. "Everything was going as we'd planned until you came along and spoiled it."

"You're a thorn in our sides, mister, and that's no lie," Theresa said.

Ruby looked at Cullen. "What are you waiting for? He's right there."

The tall man's pards looked at him, too.

"Do we or don't we?" one asked.

Cullen happened to notice Fargo's empty holster, and stiffened. "Where's his six-gun?"

"Right here," Fargo said, and quick as thought, he shot the tall man in the head. Pivoting, he put lead into the second gunman, and then had to throw himself aside as the third man—and Ruby—tried to blast him into oblivion. He fired at the third man at the same instant that Ruby fired at him.

Her slug dug a furrow but he ignored it and hurtled at the Ovaro. Knocking Wendelin out of his way, he swung onto the saddle, hauled on the reins, and raked his spur.

The stallion raced into the darkness. A few shots were thrown after them but missed.

Cutting behind a tent, Fargo stopped. More shouts were breaking out. He sat there all of half a minute, then reined back toward Ruby's tent, hoping they wouldn't expect it.

Cullen and the other pair lay in spreading pools.

Awash in lantern light from inside, Wendelin had her hand to her throat and appeared to be in a daze. She looked up, thrust her arm out, and cried, "No! Please! I'm unarmed."

Fargo vaulted down and burst into the tent, only to find it empty. Barreling back out, he grabbed Wendelin by the front of her dress and shook her. "Where are they? Where did they go?"

"They ran off," Wendelin stammered. "Theresa was scared to death. She said there's no stopping you."

"Which way?"

A crafty gleam came into Wendelin's eyes. "That way," she said, and pointed to the north.

Forking leather, Fargo rode south.

"Wait!" Wendelin cried. "What are you doing?"

Fargo brought the stallion to a trot. He had one chance, and he would be damned if he'd let them get away again.

Up ahead, two figures flitted like moths, running as if their very lives depended on it.

Against every instinct he had, Fargo slowed. Keeping them in sight was a challenge but he stuck at it for what seemed an eternity. The last of the tents fell behind them but the pair didn't stop.

The next moment, they vanished.

Reining up, Fargo alighted. A bubble of pale light suggested where they had gone. Stalking forward, he came on a dry wash. The light came from around the next bend. He flattened when he got there. From the way the light flickered and danced, it had to be a campfire.

It was.

A boy of twelve or so sat poking a stick at the flames. Behind him were Ruby's and Theresa's mounts and their pack animals. The women were just walking up to him. Jumping to his feet, the boy greeted them with a smile. "You're back later than you said you'd be."

"We're here, aren't we?" Ruby said. Taking out a poke, she flipped a coin at him, which he deftly caught. "There's your double eagle. Now get the hell gone and don't look back."

"What's wrong, lady?" the boy asked. "Why are you so mad?"

"Didn't you hear me?" Ruby gripped him by the arm and practically threw him toward Gold Gulch. "Go. And thank your ma for me for letting you stand watch."

The boy hugged the coin to his chest and dashed up out of the wash.

"Why were you so mean to him?" Theresa said. "He was only doing what we asked him to."

"Use your damn head," Ruby barked, moving to the horses. "Help me untie them. We're making ourselves scarce while we still can."

"What's your rush?" Theresa said. "We're safe. The scout has no notion of where we are."

"Fine. Then you stay here. But I'm getting the hell out while the getting is good." Ruby tugged at the picket pin a packhorse was tied to.

"I've never heard of anyone so hard to kill," Theresa said. "He should have been dead several times over by now."

"Tell me something I don't know," Ruby said. "Everyone we sent at him is dead, and I don't aim to join them."

Ruby moved to the next pack animal.

"I can't wait to get to Tucson," Theresa said. "He'll never find us there. And once we split up, we can stop worrying."

"I won't feel safe until I reach San Francisco," Ruby said.

"It's New Orleans for me."

Fargo didn't wait any longer. He hurtled around the bend and was on Theresa before she could blink. He slugged her, hard, full on the chin, and she dropped like a sack of rocks.

As fast as he'd been, Ruby was going up the other side, scuttling like a four-limbed crab. She reached the rim and pointed her revolver.

Not taking his eyes off her, Fargo dived. Instead of shooting, she bolted. He was up again in a heartbeat and flew after her into the chaparral. The pale starlight revealed her fleeing form, and damn, she could run.

Her revolver cracked.

Fargo veered but didn't break stride. The odds of her hitting him were slim. Gradually he gained, to where he could hear her panting, hear the crunch of her shoes and the crack of twigs.

Then Ruby tripped.

Fargo saw her go down. A few more bounds and he reached her as she was rising. An inarticulate snarl of rage was torn from her throat, and she barreled at him, raking with her nails, trying to claw his eyes. He realized she had dropped her revolver, and raised his to club her. She kicked his knee, throwing him off balance. She kicked his other knee, and his legs buckled. Before he knew it, he was falling.

A blow to his wrist sent the Colt pinwheeling. He blocked a punch but couldn't stop her from clawing his neck.

Ruby was beside herself, her face a twisted mask of unbridled hate.

Screaming like a mountain lion, she fought as fiercely as any man.

Fargo tried to heave her off but she clung on. She lunged at his throat, her mouth wide to bite. Somehow he got an arm up and she bit that, instead. A sledgehammer, or her knee, connected between his legs, causing the stars to spin in their orbits.

It occurred to him that he was holding back again. Unless he did something quickly, she would open a vein, or blind him.

Fargo chopped his fist at Ruby's chin. She was jarred, but redoubled her attack, her eyes glowing with twin fires bordering on madness. She had cast off every civilizing influence in her life and was as feral as a rabid wolverine. She would kill or be killed. There was no middle ground.

Fargo punched her cheek, provoking a howl of fury. He shoved, and she fell to one side. Scrambling after her, he got an arm around her waist and tried to pin her. Nothing doing. She was as slippery as an eel. She got free, and skittered a short way. He went after her. Too late, he saw her clutch something. A metallic glint told him what. He swatted her forearm as the revolver went off, practically in his face. His ears ringing, he clamped his hand to her wrist.

"Kill you!" Ruby screeched.

Deflecting another knee to his groin with his leg, Fargo slammed her to the earth.

She butted her forehead against his chin, and his teeth crunched. With a superhuman effort, she got both hands on the six-shooter and attempted to point it at his chest. He used both hands, too, trying to stop her.

Face-to-face, they battled.

Ruby suddenly spit in his eye. Inadvertently, it loosened his grip, and the muzzle brushed his ribs. Without thinking, he wrenched and shoved the barrel at her—just as the revolver went off.

Ruby gasped, and sagged.

Tearing the revolver from her, Fargo rose to his knees. "You almost had me," he panted.

A bubbling sound came from Ruby's chest. She had been lung shot. Froth spewed from her mouth as she managed to raise her head. "Damn all men, anyhow," she rasped, and died.

Fargo sat back. He hurt all over, and was bleeding from his cheek and neck and arm. The wound in his side was bleeding, too. He sat there, recovering, until his head stopped pounding and his breathing returned to normal. About to get up, he looked at the revolver. It was his Colt.

On leaden legs he returned to their campfire. He was so exhausted, he didn't look up until he stepped into the light. Surprise rooted him in midstride. "What the hell?" he blurted.

The boy was back, standing by the fire with tears streaming his cheeks. "Don't hurt me," he pleaded. "Please don't hurt me."

"Why would I?" Fargo said. "What are you doing here? You should be with your folks."

"I heard a ruckus," the boy said. "I came back and saw the one lady on the ground. I was going to help her but he stopped me."

Only then did Fargo realize Theresa was gone. "He?" he said.

The boy looked fearfully about and shook from head to toe. "An Apache. He came out of nowhere. Scared me so bad, I about wet myself. I couldn't move, couldn't hardly think."

"Slits Throats," Fargo said to himself. Just when he thought it was over. "What did this Apache do?"

The boy swiped at his eyes with his sleeve. "He . . . he put a knife to my throat. Said I was to stay here and give you a message. That if I ran off, he'd find me and slit me from ear to ear."

Fargo scanned the wash but saw no one. He listened but heard nothing. "What did he want you to tell me?"

"He said that you can keep your hundred dollars. And you can keep the horse, too."

"Hell," Fargo said.

The boy was still shaking. "Then he said a strange thing. He said his pa'd had one, and he'd always wanted one of his own. But he didn't say what it was. Then he said"—and the boy swallowed—"he said I was to thank you."

"For what?"

"For the little half-breeds they're going to bring into the world. What did he mean, mister? What was he talking about?"

"Go home, boy," Fargo said.

"Will she be all right? He won't hurt her, will he? She was always nice to me, nicer than that other one, and . . ."

"She'll be fine. Go home. Now," Fargo said.

The boy departed, a streak of misery crying softly.

Fargo did the opposite. He threw back his head and laughed long and hard. If anyone had heard him, they'd have thought he was loco.

But that was all right.

So was the rest of the world.

No other series packs this much heat!

THE TRAILSMAN

Follow the trail of Penguin's Action Westerns at
penguin.com/actionwesterns

S310

National bestselling author
RALPH COMPTON

"A writer in the tradition of Louis L'Amour and Zane Grey!" —*Huntsville Times*

Available wherever books are sold or at
penguin.com   S543

GRITTY WESTERN ACTION FROM
USA TODAY BESTSELLING AUTHOR

RALPH COTTON

GUN COUNTRY
FIGHTING MEN
HANGING IN WILD WIND
BLACK VALLEY RIDERS
JUSTICE
CITY OF BAD MEN
GUN LAW
SUMMERS' HORSES
JACKPOT RIDGE
LAWMAN FROM NOGALES
SABRE'S EDGE
INCIDENT AT GUNN POINT
MIDNIGHT RIDER
WILDFIRE
LOOKOUT HILL
VALLEY OF THE GUN
BETWEEN HELL AND TEXAS
HIGH WILD DESERT
RED MOON
LAWLESS TRAIL
TWISTED HILLS
SHADOW RIVER
DARK HORSES
GOLDEN RIDERS

Available wherever books are sold or at
penguin.com